# The Cursed Apple Tree

J. A. MILLER

Copyright © 2024 J. A Miller

All rights reserved.

ISBN: **9798877532632**

## DEDICATION

Dedicated to Jackson and Zoe Kodet who inspired the chicken coop scene.

# ACKNOWLEDGMENTS

Special thanks to my darling husband, Tim. I couldn't do this without your love and support.
Also thanks to the kids at my church, my grandkids, and nieces and nephews who kept me on task by constantly asking when the next book was going to be finished.

# 1

"We're here," Dad sang out as he pulled the van into the driveway. "Home sweet home." I looked up from my book and out the window at the new house we were moving into.

"Are we finally getting our own rooms?" I asked looking out at the three-story house.

"Not quite," Dad said putting the van in park. "Doug, Gary, and Sunny get their own room. You'll still be sharing with Baxter and Sylvester will share with Dennis."

"That's not fair," I protested. "I'm older than both Baxter and Sunny. Why can't they share a room?"

"You know why," Dad said with a sigh. "Also, you're only forty-five minutes older than Baxter." He ran a hand through his black hair and turned and looked at me daring me to continue arguing. I glared back at him but said nothing for a moment.

"Fine," I grumbled. "Whatever." Of course, I knew why Sunny got his own room. The poor kid was allergic to just about everything and his immunity system was so terrible that he got sick easily. Having his own room made it easier for him to quarantine away from my brothers and me and helped keep him sanitized.

I climbed out of the van and waited for the other two vehicles that had parked behind us to empty out. Mom had parked behind us and had Sunny, Dennis, Grandma, and Doug in her car. Uncle Hunter had been driving the other van and was behind her. He, Gary, and Sylvester got out and looked up at the new house.

Everyone in my family has dark black hair. And almost all of us have round faces. Only Grandma, Gary, and Sylvester had thin long faces.

"I've already placed flags in the house and labeled everyone's rooms," Mom said loud enough for everyone to hear. "Let's get the vehicles unpacked and out of the way before the moving trucks arrive." We immediately converged on the van Dad and I had been in since it was closest to the house. When Mom gives orders, you don't stop to argue. "Just leave the boxes in the front entrance here and I'll take care of them while we're waiting for the trucks." Mom called out as we approached the front door.

None of us kids had been in the house yet. Mom, Dad, Grandma, and Uncle Hunter were the only ones to have seen it. We didn't even get to pick our own rooms, Mom always picked those for us. It's really annoying. Usually, the room she ends up picking for Baxter and me is perfect for us, but I'd still like to have a choice.

With seven kids between the ages of eight and sixteen and four adults, the vehicles were emptied out in no time. Mom stayed in the front entrance and started taking boxes to their proper rooms. Mostly bathrooms.

My brothers and I are Army Brats. We've moved about every two years or so for as long as I can remember.

This move was special. This was our last move. Dad had been talking about retirement for the last five years and had asked us all what we wanted in our forever home. We lost no time in making plans for different projects we wanted to take on.

Doug and I wanted chickens and a place where we could experiment with self-sufficiency. I liked looking at the plans for rain collectors and garden layouts.

Mom wanted a place to make some of her own soap and do some canning. Imagine having all the green beans you want anytime you want them. Green beans are my favorite vegetable. She also promised to teach me to make my own pickles if I grew cucumbers. What can I say, I lead with my stomach.

Baxter wanted some goats. I'm not sure why, but that's what had given Mom the idea to make the goats milk soap since that was the one kind of soap that didn't cause Sunny to break out. I wasn't sure what my other brothers wanted.

Grandma and Uncle Hunter wanted to be close to us. We traveled so much and spent so much time away from where they lived that once Dad finally retired, they were planning on living close to wherever we settled. Mom had suggested that we just get a house big enough for all of us.

When we finished, Dad ordered some pizzas for lunch while Mom finished moving the boxes to their respective bathrooms. Apparently there were nine of them, because all the bathroom boxes had the same color sticker, and

## THE CURSED APPLE TREE

each sticker had a number between one and eight.

"Why do you always make our room red?" I asked looking at the last box.

"It's your favorite color." Mom answered.

"No it isn't," I said. "My favorite color is yellow."

"Are you sure?" Mom asked.

"My favorite color is red," Gary said. "And don't complain, Gil, she marked my room with pink flags."

"That's not your favorite color?" Mom asked.

"It's mine." Baxter said softly.

"Sorry boys," Mom said picking up the last box. "It's hard to keep all your favorites straight sometimes."

"That's okay," I said. "You remember our birthdays right?" Mom stopped and looked around at us all for a moment. We all started laughing.

"That's what I have your father for." Mom said smiling and leaving the front entrance.

"Can we see the rest of the house now?" Doug asked.

"Not yet," Dad said. "I want you boys to explore the grounds first. "You'll have plenty of time to see the house when we're moving things in from the trucks. If they ever get here. Let's take these pizza boxes out to the fire pit. It's about twenty feet from the back door."

We followed Dad through the house to the back door. He pointed out the living room, a bonus room, the dining room and the kitchen and a bathroom as we passed through.

"Can I have this area?" Sylvester asked looking around the fire pit.

"This is where you want to put your oasis?" Dad asked.

"Oasis?" I asked.

"Yeah," said Sylvester. "My project is going to be making an oasis where we can all sit and relax."

"Of course it is," Gary said rolling his eyes. "Why am I not surprised." I nodded.

Sylvester is the laziest person in my whole family. He can't be bothered to work at anything except for how to get out of work. He moved quickly when Mom blew the whistle though.

It was a house rule that even Grandma and Uncle Hunter jumped on board with. Blowing the whistle was the easiest way to gather all of us together no matter where we were in the house. When Mom blew the whistle you went to her. You never wanted to be the last to arrive, but I almost always was.

We had a first come, first serve rule. The first to arrive for the whistle blast got first choice of chores, food, or seat. Sylvester was usually the first to arrive so that he got served his food first, the easiest job, and the most comfortable seat. Even with the easiest job, he took forever to complete it since finishing meant he'd have to help whoever wasn't done.

"I want to put a grill over here, and definitely want to rebuild this firepit." Sylvester said.

I had to agree with him on the firepit. It was nothing more than a charred bit of ground surrounded by broken bits of cinderblocks.

"Where's my area?" Gary said looking around.

"Over there," Dad said pointing to a building. "It's the old apple barn. It'll make a perfect wood shop." Gary started walking over to the building he pointed to.

"I'm going to check out my outbuilding," Uncle Hunter said stroking his beard. "Time to start making plans." He walked so quickly that his long hair flew out behind him.

"Come on Gil," Grandma said pulling her own long hair into a ponytail and walking in the direction Gary had gone. "I'll show you where the apple trees are. There's a good place over there for your chickens."

"I'll come too," Sunny said. "There might be a good place for our gardens. I want to have an herb garden."

"You coming Baxter?" I asked.

"No," Baxter said. "I think my goats should be away from the gardens."

"I think I know a place we can put them." Dad said. He led Baxter in the opposite direction. Dennis started heading back to the house.

"Wonder if Dennis chose a project yet." Sunny said.

"Who would know?" I asked. At eight, Dennis was the youngest in the family. He'd learned how to talk, but then one day, he just suddenly stopped. Mom and Dad took him to doctors and therapists, and a number of specialists. There wasn't anything wrong with him, he just didn't speak much. He finally told a therapist that the reason he didn't speak anymore is because he just didn't have anything to say.

"Woah," I said when we got to the apple trees. "How many do you think there are?" A lot. There were a lot. Grandma looked around at the orchard.

"I don't know," she said. "Maybe two hundred or so. It's not unusual to have about a hundred trees an acre. Especially if it was the family's main source of income."

"How many acres do we have?" Doug asked.

"Altogether, it comes to about twenty-one acres." Grandma said narrowing her eyes as she looked over the trees. "But I think the apple orchard only sits on two or three acres."

"Who's going to take over the apple trees?" Sunny asked.

"I will," Grandma said her thin lips turning up into a smile causing her to look a bit sinister. "Do you boys want to help?" Doug and I looked at each other and at all the apple trees. It would be a lot of work.

"We get some of the apple stuff we produce, right?" asked Doug.

"I think that's only fair." Grandma said. "Maybe a jar for every tree?" I tried to picture what two hundred jars of cinnamon apple sauce would look like.

"We're going to need a place to store all of our food." I said.

"Mom's already working on it," Sunny said. "She's called dibs on the garage since Dad doesn't plan on using it for anything."

"Where are we going to put the vehicles?" I asked.

"We're not living in the city anymore," Grandma laughed. "We can leave them in the drive or park them in the yard."

"Don't some canned foods need to be stored in a place that's more climate controlled?" Doug asked.

"Yes," Grandma said. "But the garage has a door that leads down to a root cellar."

"I think I'd like to put my herb garden over closer to the house." Sunny said.

"What do you want an herb garden for anyway?" I asked.

"Some herbs are good for some of my ailments, and I might be able to get off of some of the chemical medicines I have to take now," Sunny said. "A lot of the medication I take is to deal with side effects of the other medication I take. But if I can use an herb that will take care of one thing without causing a side effect, I might be able to get healthier and not have to stay inside all the time."

"Well, maybe you should stick close to the apple trees," I said. "An apple a day keeps the doctor away, and with this many apples, you may never have to see a doctor again."

"If only." Grumbled Sunny.

I saw a spot that would be perfect for the garden we wanted to plant and started walking over to it. I was nearly there and about to call out to Doug when we heard the blast from Mom's whistle.

"I guess the moving trucks are here." Grandma said turning to go back to the house. I turned to follow her and my brothers when something flew by me just missing my head. Whatever it was hit Sunny right between the shoulders.

"Ow!" Sunny cried out. He turned to see what had hit him. It was an apple. "What'd you do that for?" Sunny asked me.

"I didn't throw it," I said whipping around to look behind me. "It barely missed my head."

"Where'd it come from?" Doug asked coming to stand next to me. I pointed to where I'd been looking. Near the apple trees were some woodlands and I was looking right into them. Doug raised himself to his full height and squared his shoulders before stepping purposefully into the woods.

"Doug," Grandma said. "Be careful." I stepped back to where she and Sunny stood and waited listening to the sound of Doug moving through the woods.

"No one here," Doug said. He emerged a few

minutes later. "I don't know who threw it, but they seem to be gone now."

"Think we should tell Dad?" I asked.

"Yeah," Doug said. "Later. Right now, let's get the trucks unloaded.

# 2

Four U-Haul trucks driven by some of Dad's Army buddies were lined up along the side of the road. Dad was guiding the fifth moving truck as it backed up the driveway to the house.

"You two get to unload the trucks." Mom said tying a red scarf around her shoulder length hair. It wasn't long enough to tie up, but it wasn't short enough to stay out of her face. Every time she tied her hair back, I was thankful that Dad kept my brothers and my hair cut in an Army buzz.

"Three," Sunny said. "All three of us got here at the same time." Mom looked at Sunny for a moment.

"I don't think…" Mom said.

"Let him try, Bianca," Grandma said. "You

can't protect him forever."

"It's going to be really hot in the truck," Mom said. "It might be better if he were inside with me."

"He'll be fine, Mom." I said. "Besides, it'll go faster with his help."

"And he'll be with us," Doug said. "We won't let anything happen to him."

"If he ends up having to go to the hospital for heat stroke or something like that..." Mom started.

"We'll be held responsible." Doug and I said together. Sunny was the only one the whistle rule didn't apply to. Mom always tried to reserve the easiest jobs for him, and always fixed him a plate at mealtimes before sounding the whistle.

Mom gave the others their marching orders. Since the adults were the only ones to have seen the entire inside of the house, they were stationed at different points to guide the others to where to put the boxes and pieces of furniture. Grandma got sent to the second floor. Uncle Hunter was sent to the third and Mom went into the depths of the first floor. Dad manned the entry way and would tell the others which way to go with each item or box.

It only took us an hour to get the first truck

unloaded with Dad's buddies helping. It was pretty easy since it mostly contained boxes for either Sunny, Gary, or Doug's room. Their beds and dressers were towards the back.

We'd just handed off Doug's dresser to Baxter and Gary when Dad came out and shoved a bottle of water into Sunny's hand.

"Drink." He said. He turned and shoved a bottle into my hand and then Doug's. Doug downed half his water and then poured the rest over Sunny's head.

"Thanks." Sunny sighed happily.

"Having fun?" Dad asked chuckling.

"A blast." Sunny said leaning against one of the porch columns.

"Sit," I told him. "Mom will freak if she thinks you're not resting enough."

"She'll freak if she sees him sitting down." Doug said rolling his eyes.

"You shouldn't talk about your mother behind her back." A voice behind us said causing us to jump. Grandma was standing in the doorway grinning at us.

"You gave us a heart attack," I said. "You sound just like Mom."

"Makes sense," Grandma said coming out onto the porch with us. "She is my daughter."

"How's it going out here?" Mom asked

popping her head out at us.

"Fine," Dad said. "I'm about to get the next truck."

"Bring it on," Sunny said brightly. "We're ready."

"I don't know…" Mom said slowly as she took in Sunny's appearance.

"It's just water." Dad said reassuringly.

"If he's getting hot enough to pour water over himself…" Mom started.

Doug poured it on him," Dad said. "He wanted make sure he wasn't getting overheated."

"Don't worry so much, Bianca," Grandma said. "The boys are doing a great job looking after him and Sunny was just telling me how much he was enjoying working with his brothers." Sunny gave Mom a big smile and nodded his head vigorously.

"Alright…" Mom said. "If you get too hot make sure you come find me."

"The one you really need to worry about is Dennis," Dad said. "If he's found Sunny's markers…" Mom's eyes went wide, and she ducked back into the house. Dad went to guide the next truck into place.

"You're sure you're okay?" Grandma asked Sunny. His face was pretty red.

"Just fine," Sunny said giving her a genuine smile. I couldn't help smiling too. Like I said, I'm always last to the whistle. I knew I'd get stuck unloading the truck because I usually do on moving day. I always get jobs no one else wants. But unloading the truck has its benefits. You get to take a break between each truck. The ones taking everything into the house never got a break.

"Work quickly," Dad said coming back to us. "The faster you work, the more your mother will let Sunny stay with you. The longer it takes, the more likely he'll be put on wall duty."

Sunny nearly choked on his water and looked at us with panic in his eyes. Doug downed another bottle of water and tossed it aside. I tossed mine over to where his bottle landed.

"No problem," I said. "Come on you guys, we got this." Sunny downed his own water and crushed the bottle before tossing it to our pile.

Dad estimated around an hour per truck, but his threat of scrubbing walls seemed to have lit a fire under Sunny and we managed to empty the other three trucks within two and half hours.

Doug used the time between each truck to pour water on Sunny and make sure we were both were drinking enough. Sunny seemed to be having the time of his life. I hadn't seen him smile like that since he was a baby.

"That's it," Dad said taking the last box from Sunny and handing it to Baxter. "Not for you, Dennis. Keep going." Dennis scowled and turned back to the kitchen wall.

"You can be mad all you want," Mom said. "But you earned it all on your own." Mom had taken him off box carrying duty after the first truck. He had indeed found Sunny's markers and had immediately put them to work earning him the first round of wall scrubbing duties. Mom was monitoring him and making sure he wasn't staying in one spot or skipping spots as he was prone to do.

"I'll order food." Dad said.

"Something other than pizza." Mom said.

"I saw a Chinese place when we came through town," Uncle Hunter said. "Why don't I take these three with me to get something?" He gestured to Doug, Sunny, and me.

"Good idea," Mom said glancing at Sunny. "Make sure the AC is on."

"And let Sunny sit in the front," I said. "That way he can get the full blast of the AC."

"You know what I need?" Doug said sinking back into his seat when we got into Uncle Hunter's car. "A nice hot bath to soak in."

"Your room has its own bathroom," Uncle Hunter said. "Which means you won't have to wait for anyone."

"You get your own bathroom too?" Sunny asked.

"All the adult rooms have their own bathrooms. Doug has a bathroom in his and Sunny has a half bath in his."

"That makes sense," I said laying my head back against my seat and enjoying the AC. "It'll be easier to keep Sunny's bathroom sanitized if he doesn't have to share with six other boys. Especially Dennis."

"I'm going to get my room unpacked tonight," Doug said nudging my arm. "You can soak in my tub while I unpack, and then I'll soak after that."

"Thanks." I said stretching my legs out.

"How many bathrooms does this house have anyway?" Doug asked.

"Nine." I said automatically.

"Actually, aside from the personal bathrooms," Uncle Hunter said. "There's a common full bath on each floor. One in the mother-in-law wing… nine and a half."

"Where's the half?" I asked while doing the math.

"Sunny has a half bath in his room. There's a

full bathroom in the basement," Uncle Hunter said. "It's a mostly finished basement. The only part that isn't finished is this one large closet with cinder block walls and shelves and concrete floor. Don't know if your parents have any plans for the closet itself, but the finished part they're talking about turning into a common area for you boys."

"Does it really matter if anyone does anything with it?" I asked. "We all have our projects that we're doing, I doubt anyone will care if it just stays a dank empty closet."

"Maybe," Uncle Hunter said. "You know how your mother is. She can't stand any space in a place not being used. Who knows? Maybe she'll get so involved with your canning and soap making that she won't have time to think about it."

Mom did not end up forgetting about the closet, but she never got a chance to make plans for it. Even as we were driving to pick up food, one of my brothers had snuck down to the basement, found the closet and was already silently claiming it for his own project.

# 3

I was startled awake by a whistle blast. In the glow of our nightlight, I saw Baxter immediately jump up and start dressing in clothes he'd laid out the night before. He'd actually unpacked all of his clothes last night after dinner and had them put away already. Mine were still in boxes.

"What time is it?" I asked looking at the bedroom window. Through bleary eyes, I could see that it was still dark out.

"Five," Baxter said glancing at his alarm clock. "You'd better hurry if you want breakfast."

"I don't want breakfast," I groaned pulling the covers back over my head. "I want sleep."

"Too bad so sad," Baxter said using one of

Mom's favorite lines. "We have a whole house to unpack."

"So what?" I grumbled tossing the blankets aside. "We worked our butts off yesterday. Everything's in the house. It's not the end of the world if everything isn't in its proper place by the end of the week."

"Suit yourself," Baxter said shrugging his shoulders and putting on his shoes. "I'm not getting stuck with the kitchen today." Out in the halls, I could hear my brothers calling to each other and storming down the third story hall and down the stairs.

"Gotta go," Baxter said heading for the door with a panicked look in his eyes. "I wanna get the dining room today."

I thought he'd have a pretty good chance. If the others had their choices, Doug would take the bathrooms just because he didn't trust the rest of us to set them up correctly. Gary would choose the study and he'd get stuck with Sylvester since he was the only one that could keep him on task and moving.

If Sylvester had his way, he'd choose the family room and then try to take a nap on the sofa. Dennis would want to unpack the game room, and he'd need an adult with him to keep him from playing with everything he was supposed to be putting away. If my twin brother wanted the dining room, he'd probably end up getting it. The kitchen would be mine and whichever adult got put with me. I was kind of hoping for Grandma or Dad.

I'd probably still choose the kitchen if I had first choice. I'd done it so often; I could probably do it in my sleep. I probably wouldn't know where to start in any of the other rooms, honestly.

Unpacking our own stuff could take as long as we wanted it to, but we weren't allowed to do anything until all our stuff was unpacked, put away and every last box was out of our room.

Mom usually got her, and Dad's room unpacked on the second day, and then spent about a week and a half getting all the fine touches, as she called them, in place.

Since all of my brothers had a head start on me, I figured it wouldn't matter if I took some time to actually find some clothes I actually wanted to wear for the day.

I headed down the stairs and wondered who would be stuck in the kitchen with me. Mom considered the kitchen a two-person job. If none of the adults wanted to oversee the kitchen, then it would be whoever was second to last at the breakfast table.

I had hit the second floor and was about to head for the first when I passed Sunny's room and saw that he was still inside. I stepped back and peeked in. He was sitting on the floor putting on his shoes. Most of his boxes were still taped up. One was opened in the middle of the floor, and I could see his markers sitting near the top. The box Dennis had gotten into earning him wall scrubbing duty, the day before.

"You're still up here?" I asked.

"Yeah, I'm still tired from unloading the boxes last night," He looked up at me quickly. "Don't tell Mom though."

"I won't," I promised stepping into his room. "You need any help getting ready?"

"Uh, I need a belt," Sunny said turning back to his shoes. "Is everyone else downstairs already?"

"Yeah," I said pulling a box towards me and pulling the tape off. "I was just heading down for breakfast and to get ready to clean the kitchen."

"I'll help you," Sunny said. "If you want."

"Sure," I said opening the box. "Jeans."

"Nope," Sunny said. "I packed all my belts with my socks and underwear." He pulled a box towards him and ripped the tape off. I grabbed another box and opened it.

"What are you two doing?" Mom asked coming into the room.

"Sketch books." Sunny said pushing his box over towards the marker box.

"Shirts," I said pushing mine towards the jeans box. "I'm helping Sunny find his belts, Mom. We'll be down in a bit."

"Okay," Mom said. "You have kitchen today. At least I don't have to run you down on what needs to be done."

"You take the oven, and I'll take the fridge." Sunny said.

"Deal," I agreed opening another box. Paints. "I'll take the cabinets, if you take the cupboards,"

"And we can both take on the floor and pantry," Sunny said. "Jackpot!" He pulled a belt from the box he'd just opened.

"I don't know…" Mom said slowly.

"What's wrong?" Sunny said looking up at her. "Does it clash with my outfit?" I couldn't help laughing. He was wearing a grey shirt and jeans and holding a blue belt in his hands. He knew Mom wasn't commenting on his outfit.

"Is the pantry too small?" I asked.

"You could both fit in all the pantries easily

enough." Mom said allowing herself a smile.

"ALL?" Sunny and I asked in unison.

"There are three of them," Mom said. "I've got them marked. We'll use one for dry goods like pastas and oats. The second we're going to put our canned goods in, and the third we'll use for our long-term food storage."

"Make sure you have your inhaler," I told Sunny. "The pantry areas usually are pretty dusty."

"And take breaks as you need them." Mom said.

"If we clean out the fridge first," Sunny said. "We can put the bottled water in it and then we'd have cold water for the rest of the day."

"That's about all we're going to be using the fridge for today," Mom said. "We won't be doing any cooking today. With all the unpacking and moving in we'll be doing; I don't think anyone will be in the mood for cooking. Dad and Uncle Hunter grabbed breakfast sandwiches for this morning, and Grandma and I will make the lunch run. If you boys can get the kitchen done today, I'll stop and get things to make Ninja Turtle Pancakes for breakfast tomorrow morning."

"Challenge accepted!" Sunny and I said together. We raced down to the kitchen. There were plenty of breakfast sandwiches left for the two of us. Dad and Uncle Hunter had gotten so many, that we even had a few that we could wrap up and put in the fridge for later.

We had walked through the kitchen the day before on our way out to the fire pit to burn the pizza boxes, but somehow I hadn't remembered how big it was. Sunny and I ended up changing our plan slightly. He pulled all the shelves out of the fridge and handed them to me to wash while he washed the inside of the fridge.

Personally, I didn't think it needed it, but Mom insisted on everything in the house being washed vacuumed or swept, and mopped on move in day, so despite any objections we had, we did as she wanted.

Dennis had already scrubbed the walls with Mom the day before, so that was at least one thing we didn't have to do in our room. After the fridge was cleaned, I tackled the oven while Sunny cleaned out the pantry that Mom had assigned the everyday use items. Then I cleaned out the cabinets while Sunny walked along the counter cleaning the cupboards. We started on opposite sides so that he wasn't wiping anything down onto my head.

When we were done with that, we wiped the counter down and tackled the kitchen island together and then he cleaned the dry goods pantry while I cleaned the canned goods pantry. The last thing we had to do was sweep and mop the floor.

"Wow, this looks great, you guys!" Mom exclaimed coming into the kitchen with lunch. She'd found a burger place and had bags loaded with burgers and fries. Grandma came in behind her with plastic cups and a bag of two-liter soda bottles.

"There's more bags in the car." Grandma said.

"We're on it." Sunny said running out the door.

"He's not overdoing it is he?" Mom asked me.

"No," I told her. "I've been keeping an eye on him and taking as many of the harder jobs as I can."

"That's my boy." Mom said. I ran out to help Sunny carry in the groceries.

"Not you," I heard Dad saying as I passed the family room. Dennis had just made it to the doorway when Dad called him back. "We keep working until the lunch whistle." Dennis scowled and stormed back into the family room.

True to her word, Mom had gone grocery shopping for the perishable food that would need to go into the fridge and freezer. She'd even gotten a new box of food coloring.

"Ninja Turtle Pancakes for tomorrow!" Sunny squealed happily.

"Nice!" I said giving him a high five. It took us three trips to the car to get all the groceries and put them away while Mom and Grandma set out the food, drinks, cups, and plates.

"Ears." Mom said when we were all finished. Sunny, Grandma, and I plugged our ears as Mom put the whistle to her lips. The only time I ever get to the whistle blast first for meals is when we're moving in. Like I said, there were benefits to taking the worst jobs.

Mom had apparently taken a lesson from Dad and Uncle Hunter. There were four cheeseburgers for each of us, and all the fries got poured onto three cookie sheets and placed on the kitchen island where we were all gathered to eat. We just put handfuls of fries onto our plates. Grandma operated the drink station and refused to give any refills until the person asking had eaten at least one cheeseburger. She even refused to give Mom a refill until she'd finished a burger which was amusing to us kids.

After lunch, Mom rushed the others out of the kitchen and helped us get lunch cleaned up. The fries had all been devoured and there were four cheeseburgers left over that Sunny and I tossed into the fridge next to the breakfast sandwiches while Grandma capped up what remained of the sodas.

"Alright," I said once the kitchen was cleaned again. "Our turn to kick you guys out."

"Yeah," Sunny agreed. "We want our Ninja Turtle pancakes."

"I should label the cupboards and cabinets." Mom said looking around.

"Mom, it's me," I said. "I've done this like a million times. I know where you like things to be in relation to the appliances."

"Alright, alright," Mom laughed raising her hands in the air in defense. "I'll leave you to it. I need to make sure Sylvester hasn't slipped off somewhere anyway. He got stuck with bathrooms with Doug and obviously, Doug can't be with him all the time."

"Why didn't you put him with Gary?" I asked.

"Gary's in the study, with Hunter. Hunter felt that he'd just get in the way, and I was afraid he'd actually let him slip off."

I put Sunny on the task of opening boxes while I labeled the drawers, cupboards, cabinets and pantries. Then we put the opened boxes near their respective new homes and started unpacking them. We were just breaking down the last box when Uncle Hunter and Gary came in with dinner. Fried chicken, potato wedges and a huge thing of mac and cheese and another of corn. Sunny and I pulled the sodas out of the fridge while Grandma got the plates and cups back out.

"Well," Mom said looking around the kitchen. "A deal is a deal. Ninja Turtle pancakes for breakfast tomorrow morning."

"What's a Ninja Turtle?" Uncle Hunter asked as my brothers and I all cheered.

# 4

I woke up in my new room looking up at the ceiling. Something had woken me, but I was still half asleep. I looked over at the alarm clock beside my bed. It was two in the morning. I looked over to Baxter's bed across the room. He was fast asleep and muttering something about a football truck. I figured since I was already awake, I may as well use the restroom before trying to go back to sleep and I threw my blankets aside and got out of bed.

It wasn't until I was making my way back to my room that I heard what it was that had woken me up. Mom was moving around quickly on the floor below.

"We need the bucket." Mom said.

"I don't know where it got put." Dad said.

"I put it in the pantry for the canned goods," I said quietly as I walked down to the second floor to join them. "I'll go get it."

"Quickly," Mom said. "Sunny's really sick. I knew I shouldn't have let him work in the kitchen." I hurried as quietly as I could to the kitchen and retrieved the bucket for Mom. She placed it by Sunny's bed. He was curled up on his bed groaning miserably.

"Where does it hurt?" I asked as Mom rushed back out of the room to get medicine.

"Head, tummy and here." Sunny groaned motioning to his whole stomach and abdomen.

"You're cramping up again?" I asked. He nodded pathetically. "Mom's right, you overdid it. You bent down too much." I sat down on his bed and rubbed his back.

"Here, take this," Mom said handing me a glass of water and some pills. I recognized them as children's Tylenol. She helped Sunny into a sitting position, and I handed the pills to him. He took them and then took the water from me to wash them down with.

"Is he too old for children's Tylenol?" I asked Mom.

"He shouldn't be," Mom said looking at the bottle closely. "He's not twelve yet."

"Sunny, what did you pack your warmie

with?" I asked looking around at the boxes he still had to unpack.

"Shirts," Sunny said. He pointed to a box. "Over there." I got off the bed and looked through the box. It didn't take long for me to find Maestro, the rice filled moose that we put in the microwave for when Sunny starts cramping up.

I took Maestro down to the kitchen and tossed him into the microwave for two minutes.

"Having a midnight snack?" Uncle Hunter asked coming into the kitchen.

"Sunny's not feeling well again, so I'm heating Maestro up for him." I explained.

"You're a good brother," Uncle Hunter said digging in the fridge. "Want some?" he asked coming out with some chicken dinner leftovers.

"Sure," I said. "I'll be back down when I'm done with Sunny." I poured a glass of ginger ale for Sunny as well. That's what Mom always gives us when we have an upset stomach.

It took three more days to get everything unpacked. Baxter and I unpacked Sunny's room for him as he directed us from his bed.

On our first Saturday at the new house, Sunny was finally well enough to be considered normal again. Mom and Grandma were still figuring out where to put all the decorations. Gary said he had to do some research for his project which meant that he and Dad had started to settle into the study. Uncle Hunter had started exploring the woods which Mom said were part of our property. Dennis had taken root in the library and seemed to be obsessed with reading. Baxter had started building a pen and shelter for his future goats. Sylvester spent a lot of time out by the firepit measuring and drawing.

Doug, Sunny, and I spent a lot of our time out in the yard looking for the best places for the gardens.

"I did some research, and since it's late July, we should plan a winter garden." Doug said.

"If we're planting in the summer, wouldn't it be a summer garden?" I asked.

"A winter garden implies that you're harvesting just before the winter," Doug said. "We would plant stuff that's a bit hardier and can handle the cooler weather as it's coming through."

"Okay," I said. "What are winter vegetables?"

"Lettuce, Kale, and other leafy greens can be planted now," Doug said. "We can also plant carrots, pole beans, and brussels sprouts."

Sunny and I looked at each other with matching looks of disgust.

"Do we have to plant every winter thing?" I asked.

"No," Doug said. "Not a kale fan?"

"I like kale just fine." I said.

"They're great in smoothies and salads." Sunny agreed.

"But brussels sprouts?" I asked screwing up my face.

"You don't like brussels sprouts?" Doug asked.

"They're gross." Sunny said screwing his face up as well.

"Really Gil?" Doug asked in disbelief. "You love them."

"I don't." I said.

"You do," Doug insisted. "You can't even wait for prayer before you dig into them. You shove them into your mouth before everyone else can get sit down and say the prayer."

"We pray before meals to be thankful for the food," I said. "I want to be genuinely thankful, but I don't want to thank God for the brussels sprouts, so I eat them before the prayer, so I don't have to thank him for them."

"That's brilliant." Sunny said while Doug laughed.

"Yeah," Doug said still laughing. "Real brilliant. "You're just like 'Die you devil food. No blessings for you.' You're nuts, you know that?"

"What's so funny?" Mom asked walking up to us with Grandma in tow.

"We've decided not to plant brussels sprouts." Doug said.

"That's not really fair to Gil," Mom said. "He loves them." Doug and Sunny started laughing again. I sort of felt bad, so I told Mom why I ate the brussels sprouts so fast each time.

"Gilbert Asher Blanc." Mom said scornfully.

"I'm sorry," I said. "I can't help it; I just don't like them."

"You should be sorry," Mom said with a hint of smile on her face. "I only make them so often because I thought you liked them so much. No one else likes them."

"Really?" I asked.

"Really," Mom said. "Do you know what I have to agree to just to keep your father appeased enough to eat those things?"

"Uh no." I said.

"I have to watch his stupid movies with him every time we have them. I can only take so much of Adam Sandler." Mom said.

"Adam Sandler is awesome." I said.

"His movies are stupid." Mom argued. "I swear I lose about twenty brain cells every time I watch one."

"They're funny." I argued back.

"Fine," Mom laughed. "You can make it up to me then. From now on, you watch the stupid movies with your father."

"I'm good with that." I said. Sometimes Mom misses the mark on punishments.

"So, where are you guys going to put the chicken coop?" Mom asked.

"We hadn't decided yet." Doug said.

"We're going to put the vegetable garden right here." I said walking over to the spot we'd marked off with some rocks we'd found.

"And what about the herb garden?" Mom said.

"Is it too late in the year to put one in?" Sunny asked.

"We could just build you a greenhouse and then it wouldn't matter as much," I suggested. I picked up the notebook Doug and I had been working on and turned to a blank page. "We can start by figuring out what herbs you want and then deciding on how big you want it."

"Great," Doug said rolling his eyes. "And who's going to build it?"

"I can help him," I said sitting down on the

ground. Sunny sat down next to me and looked over my shoulder. "I have an idea on how to do it and there's tons of videos online about it."

"Seriously?" Doug asked.

"How hard could it be?" I asked.

"Famous last words," Doug said throwing his hands in the air. "I'm going to help Mom find a place for the chicken coop."

"After we're done, your grandmother wants to look at the apple trees." Mom said as she followed Doug. Sunny and I waved them off as we poured over the notebook.

# 5

After we'd listed the herbs that Sunny wanted to plant and had designed the greenhouse, we decided to see if Mom and Doug had found a place for the chicken coop. We found them over in the apple orchard.

"Grandma says the apples should be ready to harvest in August," Doug said as we approached. "This one is early though." I looked up at the apple tree. Most of the trees had small green and red apples on them. The one we were standing near was the only one with large red apples.

"I wonder why this one has gone early." Sunny said.

"This is the only tree that other apple could have come from then." I said looking at the ground. There were three apples laying at the base of the tree.

"What other apple?" Mom asked absently looking around the orchard. "I think that would be a nice place for the chicken coop." She pointed to a spot about ten feet away from the tree.

"Is it a good idea to have them so close to the apple trees?" I asked.

"Why not?" Mom asked. "Most chicken farmers give their chickens scraps along with the chicken feed they get. I don't see why they wouldn't enjoy eating the apples that fall to the ground that we can't use. Then we won't have anything going to waste."

"But apples have stuff in them that are like poison to chickens." I said. "I read about it at the library in Texas when we were first talking about chickens. It's like giving chocolate to a dog."

"I'm sure we can find a place for them that's safer." Mom said. "Have you figured out where you're going to put your garden?"

"I think we first need to decide if the chickens are going to be free ranged or not," Doug said. "If they are, then we need to take into consideration how we'll protect the garden from them as well."

"You should take that into consideration anyway," Grandma said. "We have other animals in this area that will love your garden. Rabbits, deer, bears"

"BEARS?" Sunny and I asked at the same time.

"You didn't' tell us moving to Massachusetts was going to put us in bear country."

"Yeah, what if I'm allergic to bears?" Sunny asked.

"I promise that you're not allergic to bears." Mom said rolling her eyes.

"How do you know?" Sunny asked. "I've never been around one."

"Yeah," I agreed. "He's allergic to everything else."

"I'm pretty sure he's not allergic to bears." Mom said. "He's not allergic to dogs, and bears are related to the canine family."

"I'm having a hard time picturing someone taking a bear for a walk in the park." Sunny muttered.

"Or fetching a frisbee." I added.

"You're being over dramatic." Mom said turning back to where she'd indicated the chicken coop should go. Sunny and I exchanged looks. We didn't think we were being over dramatic at all. We were being just the right amount of dramatic. How does someone justify moving their kids to a place where they might be attacked at any moment by a bear without any kind of training, or instructions on what to do if you're attacked by a bear. The apple orchard was next the woods after all. Didn't bears live in woods? Or was it forests? I made a mental note to look up the difference between woods and forests.

"I think it would be best to free range the chickens," Doug said. "Since we have to fence in the garden anyway. They'll be happier that way."

"Better get a lot of them in case the bears want a chicken dinner." Sunny whispered to me.

"I'd like to get like fifty chicks." I said. Sunny, I thought, had a point. If we had plenty of chickens, it'd be a bit less devastating if a bear attacked them.

"I don't think that's possible," Mom said. "I think you have to buy them in groups of four or six."

"Okay," I said doing some quick mental math. "Then we can get... 52 chickens if they're sold by fours, and uh... sixty if they're sold in groups of six."

Doug went to stand by Mom and look over

the area she'd chosen for the chicken coop. He paced around doing his own mental math. Grandma walked over to another tree and examined the fruit it was producing.

"Look at this," Sunny said rubbing his hand over the trunk of the tree that had big red apples on it. "Someone carved something here." I looked where he was running his hands over the trunk.

"LB+MD" I said reading the engraving. "This was a sweetheart tree." The letters were big enough to see, but small enough that you might miss them if you weren't looking for them. I was impressed that Sunny had seen them at all.

"What's a sweetheart tree?" Sunny asked.

"It's a tree that two sweethearts put their initials on. Usually because it's a tree they meet at any time they want to be together. Grandma and Grandpa had one when they were younger."

"Cool," Sunny said. "Where's the tree now?"

"I don't know." I answered honestly.

"Sunny," Doug called out. "Come here, I think we found a good place for your greenhouse." Sunny walked over to where Mom and Doug were standing. I looked back at the initials carved into the tree. LB and MD. I wondered who they were.

"Ouch!" Sunny yelled out. I whipped my head around to look at what had happened.

"Gil!" Mom snapped at me. She came back to where I was standing. "Why did you do that?"

"What?" I asked. Sunny was rubbing the back of his head and looking at me with tears in his eyes.

"What?" Mom said sternly. "Don't you act stupid with me!"

"I'm not acting," I said. "What happened?"

"You know darn well what happened!" Mom said. Her face was getting red, and her mouth was trembling. "Why did you throw that apple!"

"What apple?" I asked looking around. The three apples were still at my feet. "I didn't throw any apples. I swear it."

"So, the apple just picked itself off the ground and threw itself at Sunny's head?" Mom asked in disbelief.

"I didn't, Mom! I promise. I didn't. Just like I didn't throw it the last time."

"Last time?" Mom asked looking between Sunny and me.

"The day we arrived, and we were out here looking at the apple trees," Grandma said.

"Someone threw an apple at Sunny, and it hit him in the back." Mom whirled around on me, her eyes wide with disbelief.

"I DIDN'T DO IT!" I yelled.

"Don't you raise your voice at me!" Mom said tightly.

"I HAVE TO. YOU'RE NOT LISTENING TO ME."

"No one is yelling," Mom said. "We're just trying to figure out what happened."

"Gil didn't throw it." Sunny said.

"Doug and Grandma were there too." I said calming down.

"Who threw the apple at him that time?" Mom asked Doug. Doug looked at me and Sunny helplessly.

"We don't actually know," Grandma said. Mom was eyeing me suspiciously. "It whipped by Gil's head and hit Sunny. We didn't actually see who threw it."

"Exactly," I said. "But it had to come from this tree because it's the only one with large red apples on it."

"You saw it nearly hit Gil?" Mom asked. Grandma and Doug looked at each other.

"Uh... well..." Grandma said.

"We didn't actually see anything," Doug said. "We heard the whistle and started back for the house when Sunny cried out because of the apple hitting him."

"And where were you?" Mom asked looking down at me. My shoulders slumped.

"Behind them." I said softly.

"Behind everyone?" Mom asked. I nodded. "So, we only have your word that it nearly hit you before hitting Sunny."

"But it did." I insisted.

"Enough!" Mom said turning me around and gently pushing me towards the house. "I've heard enough. Back to the house."

"Bianca," Grandma started.

"It's fine, Mother. Let me deal with this." Mom said.

She led me into the house and up three flights of stairs to my room and gently guided me inside.

"What?" I asked. "I have to wash my bedroom walls."

"If you'd like," Mom said. "I want you to do some thinking. No one saw who threw the apple the first time, and you were next to the tree this time."

"Mom, I didn't..." I started. She held up a hand.

"I'm not saying you did," Mom said. "I'm saying you were in the best position to know what happened better than the rest. So lay on your bed, wash your walls, draw, but do some thinking. Let your mind really wander over the events and then come tell me what you come up with." She turned and went back downstairs.

I looked around my room. Laying on the bed and thinking seemed the best bet. I flopped myself down on the bed and lay on my back looking up at the ceiling. I tried thinking back to our first day here, but I couldn't come up with more information than what I already had.

# 6

"Mom says to come down for dinner." Baxter said from the doorway.

"What? No whistle?" I snapped. Baxter took a step back with a look of shock on his face. "Fine. Whatever." I threw myself off my bed and Baxter jumped back to give me as much room as possible. I knew it wasn't his fault, and I shouldn't take it out of him, but I was upset I don't know why, I just was.

I stopped at the top of the steps and took a deep breath.

"Sorry," I muttered to Baxter. "It's not your fault." It was the best I could do. I'd never felt so mad before in my life. I wasn't even sure what to do with the emotion. Usually, I was the happy one. The one that could take anything with a smile. Nothing bothered me, ever.

Maybe I should talk to Gary. He's the one that's always in a bad mood and snapping at people. He's just always irritated at something. He'd know how to handle it.

I sat at my place at the dinner table between Sylvester and Dennis. Mom had just sat the last bowl of food on the table and took her own seat.

"Well, everything looks good." Uncle Hunter said. He spooned some of the beef stew onto his plate and passed it to Dad. I took some beef stew when it came my way, and some mashed potatoes.

"Skip the veggies," Doug hissed at me over Dennis' head. I took the bowl of veggies from him and looked inside. Brussels sprouts. Great, Mom really had it in for me. I scowled at the beastly things and passed them to Sylvester. He passed them to Grandma without even glancing at them. Grandma put some on her plate, and I couldn't help but see her give Mom a questioning glance.

Mom frowned at the amount of Brussels sprouts left in the bowl. It had already gone through the hands of Dad, Doug, Dennis, me, Sylvester and Grandma. The only ones that had the vegetables on their plates so far were Dad,

Dennis, and Grandma. She glanced at my plate, but I turned away from her in case she tried to catch my eye. After a moment, I saw the bowl pass to Sunny out of the corner of my eye.

Sunny put some on his plate, but he was watching me. I wanted to punch whoever threw that apple at him. I sort of hoped it was the same person that threw an apple at him the first time. Then I'd only have to punch one person. I didn't know anyone in town yet, but when I found out who was behind it…

Anyone who knew our family wouldn't really think there was anything wrong with dinner that evening. Dad and Uncle Hunter talked about the outbuilding they were going to use as their hunting lodge. Gill was glaring into his plate as usual. Doug and Baxter were discussing the chickens and goats and wondering if they would have a good relationship with each other.

"Goats can be territorial, but chickens aren't pushovers by any means," Baxter said. "It'll take them a bit to figure out that they don't have to really compete for resources. The real trouble is keeping them out of the gardens."

"You don't think a chicken wire fence around the garden would do the trick?" Doug asked.

"It might." Baxter said. "I don't know if goats can eat through it or even if they would. I'll have to look it up."

"Dennis! No!" Doug yelled suddenly grabbing Dennis' arm. Dennis had finished his first round of food and was reaching the spoon he'd been eating with into the pan of potatoes to get himself some more. "No one wants your germs!" Dennis jerked his hand back quickly and licked the back of Doug's hand. "AAuugg!"

Dennis giggled and stuck his tongue out and leaned towards Doug trying to lick him some more. I didn't really understand Doug's issue on the matter. Sure, there's germs on Dennis' spoon since he ate off of it, but we were all related to one another, did it really matter? Then I looked over at Sunny and realized that in his case, it probably did. He was grinning at Doug trying to avoid being licked by Dennis.

"Vou te lamber porque você é um pão mofado." Dennis said. It wasn't the cleverest insult, but it was funny hearing it come from Dennis. He didn't speak much, but when he did, it was usually in Portuguese.

"Vou amarrá-lo como um pretzel." Doug said putting his own spoon down so he could wrestle Dennis with both hands.

"What did he call him?" Uncle Hunter asked.

"Dennis said he was going to lick Doug because he's a moldy bread." Dad explained.

"And Doug's going to tie him up like a pretzel." Gary added. He reached his knife out for more butter at the same time Baxter did.

"On Guard," Baxter said flicking Gary's knife away with his own.

"It's en-garde, you freak." Gary said clashing his knife against Baxter's. "Who taught you French?"

"Tu l'as fait, Bozo." Baxter answered. And just like that the two were engaged in sword fight with the plate of butter as the prize. Dad looked at Dennis still fighting for the right to lick our eldest brother and to my twin and second eldest brother sword fighting with butter knives. He opened his mouth to say something, but then gave a small smile and the smallest of chuckles and went back to eating and talking to Uncle Hunter about obtaining the proper licenses for hunting in the fall.

"Gil, you've hardly touched your food," Mom said. "Everything okay?"

"No?" I snapped. Baxter and Gary both immediately stopped fighting. Everyone except Dennis and Doug went still and quiet. Dennis didn't seem to notice and was still trying to lick

Doug who gave up on eating altogether and pulled Dennis squirming onto his lap.

"What's bothering you?" Mom asked. It was annoying to listen to her talking to me like nothing had even happened.

"You couldn't be bothered to come and tell me dinner was ready." I muttered.

"I was getting food on the table," Mom said. I finally looked at her and wished I hadn't. She was wearing a hurt expression as if she were the victim. "Why are you upset?"

"I don't know," I exploded. "Maybe because my own mother thinks I'm some kind of monster who takes joy in hurting my little brother."

"Gil," Dad said warningly.

"You're upset because I sent you to your room to think through what happened to your brother?" Mom asked incredulously.

"I didn't throw that stupid Apple!" I yelled.

"Gil." Dad said more firmly.

"I can only go by what I see." Mom said.

"But you didn't see anything." I said. I'd lowered my voice, but keeping control was getting harder by the minute.

"Well, I'm sorry you feel victimized..." Mom said.

"That's not really an apology," I said cutting

her off. "I didn't throw the stupid apple. Not this time, not the last time, not ever."

"You should eat something," Mom said changing the subject. "You missed lunch."

"Because you told me not to leave my room." I muttered.

"I didn't say you couldn't leave your room. Here, I made Brussels sprouts," Mom said. "They're your favorite."

"I hate Brussels sprouts!" I said a little louder than I meant to.

"He told you that this afternoon," Doug said tightening his hold on Dennis. He grabbed Dennis' spoon from him and scooped up food from the plate that sat in front of Dennis' now empty chair. He'd managed to get Dennis into a position as if he were a baby. "Okay, Baby, time for your din din. Open wide and say ah." Dennis giggled and allowed himself to be fed.

"Sorry, Gil," Mom said. "I guess I forgot."

"Whatever," I said. "I'm not even hungry." I shoved myself back from the table and made my way upstairs back to my room.

"Gil!" Mom called after me. "Come back! Gil!"

I ignored her and continued up to my room. I shut the door behind me and sat on my bed. I knew I wouldn't be alone for long. I could already hear footsteps on the stairs, and I knew exactly whose they were. I sat on my bed defiantly waiting to face my accuser.

# 7

My door opened slowly and silently. Mom stood in the doorway red faced and breathing hard. Probably from trying to run up three flights of stairs. It always struck me how much she looked like a dragon when she was really mad.

This kind of anger was usually reserved for school admins who had somehow found fault without cause against one of us kids. I could see why they always backed down, but I met her eyes without fear. She could huff and puff all she wanted, but she couldn't intimidate me.

"Don't ever walk away from me like that again?" she said slowly. "I am your mother. I'm one of the people in your life you're supposed to be able to trust."

"You really think I threw an apple at my brother!" I yelled.

"I know an apple hit your brother, and you're the only one that had the best view of what happened." Mom said calmly.

"I didn't throw it!" I yelled.

"I didn't say you did." Mom said.

"Well, you're acting like I did!"

"ENOUGH!" Dad yelled from the doorway.

"Go back to the table," Mom said barely glancing at him. "I'm handling it."

"I know," Dad said glaring at us. "We can all hear you handling it from the dining room table three stories down."

"Sorry, Dad," I said. "I didn't realize we were being that loud." Dad stepped in and closed the door behind him.

"You're the only one being loud. Tell me what happened this afternoon," Dad said quietly. "Your own words, your own account."

I repeated to him what I'd told Mom earlier.

"And you didn't see anyone?" Dad asked.

"No, Sir," I said. "Just Grandma, Mom, Doug, and Sunny."

"Doug said someone threw an apple the first day we got here." Dad said.

"I didn't throw that one either," I said. "I just waited for the others to go ahead of me so I could be last to the whistle."

"You wanted to be last?" Mom asked.

"No one really likes to unload the trucks, so I just make myself last, so I do it and the others don't have to."

"You're always last to the whistle on purpose?" Dad asked.

"Yeah," I said shrugging. "Why?"

"I guess it just never occurred to me that you would do it intentionally." Dad said.

"I would choose to unpack the kitchen if I were first anyway, and I don't usually eat as much as the rest, so it never seemed to matter," I said.

"Hunter and I will search the woods tomorrow evening," Dad said. "We may have some homeless people living in them. Hunter's been exploring them, but I don't think he was looking for signs of camping."

"Be careful," Mom said giving me a sideways look. "If they're not above attacking kids…"

"We're going back to the dinner table," Dad said to me. "Take some deep breaths and come back down when you're ready, okay?" I nodded and the two of them left my room.

I didn't like the idea of people living in the woods trying to attack us. The very thought sent a shiver down my spine.

"Where did this come from?" I asked as Dennis passed me a bowl of green beans."

"Mom made them up while you were upstairs." Doug said. "I told her that your favorite vegetable was actually green beans."

"How'd you know that?" I asked him.

"You were insistent that they were going in our garden." Doug answered.

Grandma and Uncle Hunter were watching me closely, but Mom, Dad, and my brothers were chaotic as usual.

"I won the butter duel," Baxter said. "My sword skills were too much for him."

"More like your horrible French was too much for me." Gary muttered. I noticed he still got some butter on his second round of mashed potatoes.

"Ian and I are heading into town for supplies," Uncle Hunter said. "Anyone who needs something should let me know by the end of breakfast tomorrow morning.

"I'd better come with you," I said. "I need specific supplies for Sunny's greenhouse." Dennis started hopping in his seat with his hand in the air like he had a question.

"Yes, Dennis," Uncle Hunter said. "You can

come too."

"Doug, you and I can get the materials from the lumber yard you'll need for your chicken coop if you have it designed already." Dad said.

"I can have it ready by tomorrow morning." Doug said.

"Are you both going to the lumber yard?" Grandma asked.

"It's actually the same place. The home improvement store has a lumber section." Dad said. "Hunter's getting all the hardware and do-dads he and Gary need for their out-buildings. They have a garden center too, so the boys will be able to get what they need for their gardens."

"Sure, you want to go Dennis?" Dad asked. Dennis nodded enthusiastically.

"I'll get a list made for you tonight, Uncle Hunter." Sylvester said. "I don't really feel like walking around a home improvement warehouse or a lumber yard all afternoon. Besides. I've got some reading I need to do."

"Anyone else want to ride along with one of us?" Dad asked.

"I'll ride with Uncle Hunter," Gary grumbled. "I'll make a list, but I'd feel better if I picked out the things I wanted."

All in all, dinner ended much better than it started. I still felt uneasy as I slipped into bed that night.

# 8

I don't know what Uncle Hunter thought was going to happen taking Dennis with us. As soon as we got to the door, Dennis grabbed a cart and took off into the store. He was out of sight in less than a minute.

"Uh oh." Uncle Hunter said. "I guess we should let the staff know."

"Forget it," Gary said rolling his eyes. "He'll pop up after a bit."

"He does this often?" Uncle Hunter asked.

"Pretty much every time we take him to store," I said shrugging my shoulders. "Mom has a weird way of knowing exactly where he is though. Don't know how, but every time she'll say something like 'He's over in the books,' or 'He's looking at bikes.' And she's always right."

"We don't have your mother here though." Uncle Hunter said. Gary pulled out his phone and dialed.

"Hey, Mom," Gary said into the phone. "We're at the store, where'd Dennis go? Okay." He hung up his phone and stuck it back into his pocket. "She says to check the garden section."

"Why would he be in the gardening section?" I asked. Gary shrugged his shoulders and led the way. Sure enough, Dennis was looking at some seed starting trays.

"How could she possibly know that?" Uncle Hunter asked.

"Mom's got wicked powers," I said. "She can't remember our favorite colors, our birthdays or favorite foods, but she knows where we are at any given moment."

"And she's never called us by the wrong name," Gary said. "She knows exactly which kid she wants no matter how ticked off she gets."

"Your grandmother couldn't even do that," Uncle Hunter said. "Even though there was only the two of us, she'd yell out the name of every family member including the dog and cat before she'd finally land on whichever of us were in trouble."

"I guess our mom is just cooler than your mom." I said.

"Obviously," Uncle Hunter said looking over the seeds. "Mine never taught me other languages."

"Neither did ours," Gary said. "We were stationed in Brazil for six years, remember?"

"I do," Uncle Hunter said. "I never heard any of you speak Portuguese though."

"It's Dennis' first language," I said. "He learned it before learning English because Mom was always speaking Portuguese with the other moms at the parks."

"I suppose you picked up the French while you were stationed in France for four years?" Uncle Hunter asked.

"Gary and Doug did," I said. "They taught the rest of us."

"Baxter messes up his French just to annoy me." Gary grumbled.

"That's not hard to do," I laughed. "Everything annoys you." Dennis rounded a corner and was gone again. Uncle Hunter and Gary went back into the store for their hardware, while I stayed in the gardening department to get the stuff Doug and I would need for the garden and the things Sunny would need for the greenhouse.

Dennis kept popping in and out of view. He flew by me at one point with a planter box and a squirt bottle in his cart. There were a few other things that looked like different types of thermometers. He whipped around a corner and disappeared into the store.

After I'd gotten what I needed from the garden center, I went back into the store to look for the hardware that I'd need for fencing in the garden and constructing the greenhouse. I found Gary in the hardware area looking over organizers.

"Did you really throw that apple at Sunny?" Gary asked. "I don't actually care if you did, and I won't tell on you. I was just wondering." I knew Gary wouldn't tell on me for anything I'd done. He never told on anyone.

"No," I said. "I really didn't. I don't know what happened. I know I shouldn't have gotten so mad at Mom, but..."

"Why not?" Gary asked turning to look at me.

"She was just worried about Sunny." I said.

"So what?" Gary snapped. "You still have a right to be mad at false accusations."

"I mean, yeah..." I started.

"Look, you can't let her just get away with it." Gary said.

"What do you mean?" I asked. "Get away with what? She didn't really accuse me of anything."

"She didn't exactly believe you either." Gary said. He put his hands on his hips and sighed heavily at the ceiling. He finally looked back at me. "Look, I'm not saying you shouldn't be mad, and I'm not saying you should hold a grudge, but if you're innocent of something and someone isn't giving you the benefit of the doubt, you should hold your ground."

"I don't know," I said. "I just don't know how to do that."

"Don't you ever get tired of being in a good mood all the time?" he asked.

"I don't know," I shot back playfully. "Don't you get tired of being grumpy all the time?"

"I'm not grumpy all the time. I just act like it so Mom will leave me alone and stop expecting stuff out of me."

"Like what?"

"Like being a better role model for my little brothers." Gary snarled. "Do you know how annoying that gets after a while. Doug's the oldest, let him be your stupid role model. Why should I have to be perfect? Why can't I just be myself and do my own thing?"

"But you are a good role model," I said. Gary

huffed and turned back to the organizers. "Being yourself and doing your own thing is the best thing you can do for us. Why would we all want to do everything like Doug. No one can match him. Mr. Honor roll, and perfect attendance."

"Yeah," Gary laughed hollowly. "I've heard about that too. 'Why can't you be more like your older brother? If you slack off the others will think they can too. You need to be better for them.' I'm not your parent, I didn't ask to be born so close to the top of the order."

"She didn't actually tell you that?" I asked rolling my eyes.

"Oh yes she did," Gary grinned. "Apparently, I'm to blame for your grades."

"There's nothing wrong with my grades," I said. "I may not be on the honor roll or anything, but they're passing grades."

"What's your favorite subject?" Gary asked.

"In our old school?" I asked. "Home Ec. I like cooking and baking."

"Really?" Gary asked. "I've never seen you do either."

"Mom never lets me," I said throwing my hands in the air. "She pretty much dictates the kitchen. No one is allowed to try and cook or bake in there except her and grandma."

"Have you ever heard of a midnight snack?" Gary asked.

"Yeah…"

"Tonight. Midnight. Kitchen. Don't be late." Gary said. He walked off down the aisle.

"Aren't you getting one of these?" I asked pointing to an organizer.

"Nah," Gary said over his shoulder. "Just getting ideas. I'll be in the fasteners if you need me." I shook my head and grabbed an organizer with drawers. I planned on using them for seeds that didn't get planted.

I caught back up with Uncle Hunter and Gary. Uncle Hunter wanted to ask an attendant to call for Dennis over the intercom, but Gary just called Mom who said he was waiting for us at the register. Sure enough, Dennis was standing near the registers with his cart. Along with the seed trays, spray bottle and thermometers, he had a fifty-pound bag of compost manure, large cone shaped light bulbs, and lamps. He was looking at his watch waiting for us. He held his watch up for us to see when we approached him. It was twenty minutes past noon.

"Oh, how could we be so late for lunch?" Gary said smiling and rolling his eyes. He glanced at me. "I guess you two think with your stomachs." Dennis rubbed his tummy and licked his lips making slurping sounds.

"Lunch is on me," Uncle Hunter said pushing his cart up to a register. "And this is all on your dad."

"Where should we eat?" I asked as Uncle Hunter loaded the items in his cart onto the belt.

"I vote Mexican," Gary said. "I saw a place on the way here that looked good. I'm up for a taco salad." Dennis smiled broadly and clapped.

"I'm down." I agreed.

"Sounds good to me." Uncle Hunter said.

# 9

The alarm clock next to my bed said that it was five minutes to midnight. I got out of bed as quietly as I could and slipped out of the bedroom. Gary was just slipping out of his room when I stepped out into the hall. He put a finger to his lips and the two of us crept up to the rail and looked over. The second floor was still and quiet. There weren't even any noises coming from Sunny's room. Gary and I slipped downstairs as quickly and quietly as we could.

I flipped the switch on the wall and the light flooded the kitchen. Everything was clean and quiet. The kitchen island gleamed from where Mom or Grandma had scrubbed it after dinner. I'd never heard the kitchen so quiet before. It was really eerie.

"Okay," Gary whispered. "Where do we start?"

"Grab some apples while I grab some flour, salt, sugar, and cinnamon."

"We're making an apple pie?" Gary asked.

"We're gonna do better than that." I grabbed the flour bin and set it on the kitchen island. The sugar and salt bowls soon joined it.

"What else?" Gary asked as I pulled the cinnamon from the spice rack.

"Uh, some butter, and applesauce," I said. I looked at the assembled ingredients. "Milk. We also need milk." I grabbed some vanilla and oil.

"Are you sure we're not making a pie?" Gary asked. A squeak behind us caused us to jump and whirl around. The basement door slowly swung open and revealed Dennis standing in the doorway. The three of us stood there staring at each other trying to figure out who was more in trouble.

"What are you doing up?" I asked in a hoarse whisper. Dennis jabbed a thumb down the stairs to the basement. He stepped further into the kitchen and quietly closed the door and then walked over to the island and got onto a stool to look over the assembled ingredients.

"I need that pot," I said pointing to a large red double handled pot. Dennis jumped from his stool and grabbed it from its hook and brought it back to me. "On the stove," I told him. "It needs to be filled like a third way full of oil and heated to a simmer." Dennis placed the pot onto the stove and Gary filled it and turned on the stove.

I measured out the flour, salt, and sugar into a mixing bowl. Then I measured out the applesauce, milk, vanilla, and oil into a second mixing bowl. I slid the mixing bowl with the wet ingredients and a whisk over to Dennis who had resumed his spot on a stool. Dennis stirred the ingredients, and I handed a whisk and the dry ingredients over to Gary while I started peeling the apples.

"What are you guys doing?" a hissed whisper came from the doorway. We looked over to find Baxter standing in the doorway of the kitchen.

"What are you doing?" Gary hissed back at him.

"I woke up to use the rest room and saw that Gil was gone."

"We're making a midnight snack," I whispered. "Get over here and help me peel these apples."

"How many do we need peeled?" Baxter asked.

"Eight," I said. "I have a feeling we're going to need them."

Baxter and I had only peeled two apples when Sylvester and Sunny had joined us in the kitchen. I had Sylvester help Baxter peel the apples while I started slicing them from side to side.

"Are you guys insane?" a hissed whisper asked coming from the doorway. We looked up to see Doug standing in the doorway.

"Here," I said pushing the sliced apples towards him. "Use the small biscuit cutter to cut the star out of the center of each of these slices and toss them into the empty bowl over there. Gary, you can start putting the dry ingredients into the wet ones." Gary pulled the mixing bowl Dennis was working on towards him and started adding the dry ingredients a little bit at a time. Doug hesitated at the doorway and then after a look over his shoulder at the stairs, came into the kitchen and followed my instructions.

"What do we do after this is all mixed up?" Gary asked.

"That's the batter," I said. "We'll dip the apple rings into it and then put them three or four at a time in the oil to fry."

"What are we making?" Doug asked.

"Apple rings," I said. "Like onion rings, but with apples."

"Okay, I'm done," Baxter said setting the peeler down.

"Grab another bowl and a spoon and mix up a half a cup of sugar and a teaspoon of cinnamon. We'll use it to coat the apple rings after they come out of the oil." Sylvester pulled a large bowl out of the cupboard and lined it with paper towels.

When Gary and Dennis finished mixing the batter, Gary placed the batter on the counter next to the stove and checked the oil in the pan.

"I think we're ready to start the first round," Gary said. "How long should they be in here?"

"About two minutes on each side," I answered. "Just enough to cook the batter and make the apples nice and tender." Doug handed the bowl over to Gary who poured them into the batter and handed the bowl back to him. He used a fork to pull a ring out and gently placed it in the hot oil.

"Dennis, do you want to coat the rings in the cinnamon and sugar coating when they're done?" I asked. Dennis nodded and moved his stool over to the counter next to Gary.

After nearly an hour, all eight of the apples had been peeled, sliced, cored, battered, fried, and coated in cinnamon sugar. Baxter pulled down seven glasses and Sylvester pulled a gallon of milk from the fridge and poured us each a glass.

"Alright," Gary said rubbing his hands together. "Who's going to try them first?"

"This was your idea," I told him. "You eat the first one."

"Don't you have faith in your own recipe?" Gary asked. Dennis had reached the end of his patience and his hand shot out to grab the first ring and take a big bite from it. We all watched him for a moment as he chewed trying to decide how much he liked it. He swallowed the first bite and then closed his eyes, smiled, and rubbed his tummy.

"Good enough for me." Sunny said and grabbed a ring for himself. We each grabbed a ring and started eating. There wasn't a whole lot of talking as we ate our snack and drank our milk.

"Not bad," Gary said licking his lips. "Not bad at all."

"Yeah," Doug agreed. "Who knew Gil was so good at cooking?"

"I'm not surprised," Sylvester said. "He's been setting up the kitchen every move. He was bound to learn something."

"That doesn't mean anything," Baxter said. "But I'm not surprised either. His grades in Home Ec. are better than most of the other students in our classes."

"Don't talk too soon," Gary said. "We haven't had any classes at the Tawny Delis schools yet. He might meet his match here."

"Are you ready for the new school year?" I asked Gary. At fourteen, he was about to enter his freshmen year of High School.

"Yeah," Gary said. "At least I won't have to listen to Mom's first of the school year lecture about looking out for you two for another two years."

"Bet we'll be hearing it about Sunny," Baxter said. "He starts middle school with us this year."

"I can't wait for next year," Sylvester said glumly. "But I'll certainly get the lecture about Dennis." Dennis glared at Sylvester.

"Dennis doesn't need looking after," I said rolling my eyes. "I'd be more concerned about anyone messing with him than I would about Dennis. He's too crafty to just be bullied."

"Or if he did get bullied, he wouldn't tell you about it," Gary said. "He'd just figure out a way to get revenge on his own."

"And get away with it somehow," Doug said.

"I have no idea how he gets away with everything and somehow, if we do the same thing, we're instantly in trouble." We all looked at Dennis. Dennis just smiled innocently and finished off his glass of milk.

"Let's get the kitchen cleaned up before Mom sees it and has a conniption fit." I said. Ten minutes later we were standing in the doorway looking around the kitchen. It was gleaming just as it had been when Gary and I had just entered it at midnight.

"Now the hard part," Doug whispered. "The seven of us creeping up the stairs to our bedrooms and acting like this never happened."

"I'll go first," Sunny said. "Mom won't be so mad if she sees I'm up simply because I wanted a drink. Stay close to the wall. The stairs don't creak as much there."

"Wait," I whispered back. "How do you know?" Sunny just shot us a smile and started up the stairs.

We crept up the stairs with Sunny and Doug in the lead and Dennis bringing up the rear. Sunny made it safely to his room. Doug slipped down the hall to his own room. The rest of us were all up on the third floor.

We slipped up the next set of stairs and Sylvester slipped into his room which was closest to the stairs. Baxter and my room was next, and once we were inside our room we hung out at the doorway waiting for Dennis and Gary to get into their rooms.

"How does he move so quietly?" Baxter asked watching Dennis slip into his room.

"No idea," I said pulling myself back into the room and closing the door. "The kid moves like a shadow."

"Think that's how he gets away with stuff so often?"

"I don't know," I said climbing into bed. "He was in the basement when Gary and I went down to the kitchen at midnight, and neither of us had heard him."

"What was he doing down in the basement?"

"Dunno," I said. "Probably playing one of the video games. He is the youngest after all. He's usually the last to get a turn since we're all older and just kind of push him aside."

"We should be nicer to him." Baxter said.

"Yeah," I agreed. "Especially if we don't want to be the ones taking care of Mom and Dad when they're old."

"Still mad at her huh?"

"I guess a little," I admitted. "I just wish she believed me."

# 10

The following day, everyone was busy with projects. Doug and Dad had started building the chicken coop and the run. Gary was helping Baxter finish building the pen and shelter for his goats.

Uncle Hunter and I had made a deal. I'd help him with his hunting lodge if he helped me with the greenhouse for Sunny's herb garden.

Working with Uncle Hunter was enjoyable. He didn't take the work too seriously and we joked around as we built the frame for the greenhouse.

"Are you sure it needs to be this big?" Uncle Hunter asked as we mapped out just how we were going to lay it out.

"There's going to be like sixteen different herbs in here," I answered. "They all need a specific set of space to grow in."

"Sixteen herbs?" Uncle Hunter asked looking over the base of the greenhouse. "That's quite a bit."

"Actually, I don't think they're all herbs," I said. "I don't know if garlic, ginger, or ginseng count as herbs, and I'm pretty sure that Cinnamon and Cardamom are considered spices."

"Are they medicinal, or are some of them just for taste?"

"They're all medicinal," I said. "But they can also be used for flavoring." I pulled out the list that Sunny had made and showed it to Uncle Hunter while I finished laying out the pieces that would make up the ground frame of the greenhouse.

"Well, maybe when his herbs are ready to harvest he'll set aside some for us to use in the kitchen," Uncle Hunter said. "And maybe the next time you guys decide to sneak down to the kitchen for a midnight snack, you'll invite me."

"How'd you know about that?" I asked.

"Sylvester isn't that good at sneaking out of his room," Uncle Hunter answered. "I'm surprised your mother isn't aware of your midnight excursion."

"Why didn't you just join us?" I asked.

"Seemed like you guys were having a good time, and I didn't want to intrude on brothers bonding."

"What would your ideal midnight snack be?" I asked.

"I don't know. Maybe a chocolate chip cookie with a scoop of ice cream on top? Or maybe some loaded potato skins?"

"I can definitely do loaded potato skins." I said. I could already taste them and was just thinking about when I would dare attempt another Midnight Meeting with Uncle Hunter when we got the last of the frame in place.

"All done," Uncle Hunter said securing the last pipe. "I'll go get the covering."

"I'm gonna go see how the chicken coop is coming." I said. It only took a few minutes to get to where the chicken coop was being built.

"What do you think?" Doug said waving a hand at it. It looked pretty good. It was a large square building with a set of nesting boxes that protruded out of the left side. The front had a large door that swung up to reveal the roosting bars inside. The right side of it had a small door with a ramp that led down to the ground inside the run.

"I think it's too close to the apple trees," I said. "And I thought we were going to let them free range."

"We are," Doug said. "The run opens to the other side to let them out into the yard. We're going to fence off the apple orchard so they can't get to the apples. Mom and I think this is the best place for them though. There's also a door on this side so that we can come in and feed them without them seeing us go into the run."

"We don't want them to see us?" I asked.

"Your grandmother said they tend to follow the one that brings them the food and roosters can be a bit aggressive." Dad explained. "It's more trouble than we need to go to, but why not?"

"But if they're going to be free ranged, why do they need doors at all?" I asked.

"Just in case of bears and storms and stuff." Doug said. "If we decide to be a little overprotective, we can be."

"The run is more just a way for them to have a place to get out of the rain or the sun if they want," Dad said. "I need to get over and help Gary now that we're done here."

"I'll go see if Sylvester needs help with his oasis." Doug said. Baxter and Sunny walked up just as they were getting ready to walk away.

"Can we see the insides?" Sunny asked.

"Just make sure everything is locked up before you guys take off again," Dad said. "We don't want anything moving in before we get the chickens next spring."

"If we're not getting them until next spring, why did we build the coop already?" Baxter asked.

"So that we can see how it'll stand the fall and winter," Doug said. "This way we can fix anything as we go without the chickens being in any danger." The two walked off leaving us alone with the coop.

"Coming Gil?" Sunny asked as he and Baxter entered the door by the trees.

"Nah," I told him. "Uncle Hunter is probably ready to put the plastic cover on your greenhouse. I should get back and help him."

"Suit yourself." Sunny said climbing into the coop.

"Hey Gil," Baxter called. "Let down the big door and latch it. I want to see how dark it is in here with just this little door open." Sunny giggled and I just shook my head and followed his directions.

"Don't lock the run door though," Sunny said.

"I won't." I promised. I shut the large door and swung the latches into place before turning and rejoining Uncle Hunter.

We got the plastic cover into place and secured to the frame in no time. The shelves we'd bought for the greenhouse were easy to put together and in half an hour, we had the whole thing assembled. We were just standing back to admire our work when Mom came walking around the corner at a fast pace.

"Mom, check it out." I said gesturing to the greenhouse.

"Nice," Mom said glancing at the greenhouse. She turned to me with stern eyes and her lips pressed tight together. "Care to explain yourself?"

Uncle Hunter and I looked at each other and then back to Mom.

"Uh, do you want an invite to the midnight snack too?" I asked.

"Midnight snack?" Mom asked.

"Isn't that why you're upset?" I asked. "Uncle Hunter already got after me for not inviting him last night."

"Wait," Mom said holding her hands out and waving them. "Are you telling me you got up at midnight and made a snack?"

"Yeah," I said with a shrug. "We made apple

rings. We cleaned everything up."

"We?" Mom asked.

"Us kids." I explained.

"That explains the milk being so low," Mom said. "No, I'm talking about the chicken coop."

"What about it?" I asked.

"Locking your brothers inside?" Mom said.

"WHAT?" Uncle Hunter said turning to look at me incredulously.

"Baxter told me to." I said. "He wanted to see how dark the coop was when the large door was shut."

"Come with me." Mom sighed rolling her eyes and turning away. Uncle Hunter and I followed her back to the chicken coop.

Mom bent down and picked up a large branch and held it out to me.

"What is this?" she demanded.

"A large branch?" I asked.

"A large branch that you propped against the door and blocked shut while Sunny and Baxter were inside."

"Why would I do that?" I asked.

"I don't know!" Mom said. "Why do you do anything?"

"I don't think it was him!" Uncle Hunter said. Now he was getting heated.

"You can't know that for sure," Mom said.

"You don't know him like I do. This is exactly the kind of prank he would pull." I hate to admit it, but she was right. I'd never locked anyone in any kind of structure before, but if I thought someone was going to be coming around the coop soon, or if I thought my brothers could get out, I would definitely lock them in a chicken run.

"But I didn't." I told Mom. "I promise you I didn't."

"Well, no one else was nearby when it happened." Mom said glaring at me.

"Did you think to ask them what happened?" I asked glaring back at her.

"We got into the coop, and you closed the door." Baxter said.

"You told me to." I repeated.

"But I told you not to lock the run door," Baxter said. "You didn't even lock it with the lock bar Dad installed. You propped a whole tree branch against the door."

"No, I didn't." I insisted. "I never touched the run door. I locked the coop door and went right back to Uncle Hunter."

"Are you upset about moving here?" Mom asked. "Is that why you're acting out?"

"I'm not acting out." I said raising my voice.

"I really don't want to move again." Baxter

said.

"No!" I yelled. "You promised! You promised we wouldn't have to move again!"

"Relax," Mom said holding her hands up defensively. "No one's moving again. Trust me, I am done with the moving."

"I thought you liked moving around," Uncle Hunter said putting his hands on his hips. "Every move was exciting and a new place."

"I did what I had to do to survive," Mom said bracingly. "Blame our mother. She's the one that taught us to try to see the positive in every situation."

"Seeing the new places was cool and all," Sunny said. "But we never got to really make any friends. These guys were the only friends I ever had." He waved a hand over at Baxter and me.

"Well, that's not nice," Mom said. "How do you think that makes them feel?"

"SAME!" Baxter and I said together enthusiastically.

"We love our brothers, Mom." I said.

"Seriously, we do," Baxter said. "But we can only stand looking at them for so long."

"It's bad enough we have to look at each other as often as we do."

"I vote for a few more additions to the house

so we can finally have our own rooms." Baxter said.

"Give it another two years and Doug will be off to college." Uncle Hunter said. "Then one of you can have his room."

"Fight you for it," I told Baxter.

"No one's fighting anyone right now," Mom said.

"What's going on?" Dad asked as he and Doug walked over to the coop.

"Gil propped a tree branch against the door and locked his brothers inside the run." Mom said.

"I did not." I said. "Dad, I swear I didn't do it."

"The branch didn't just magically appear there, Gil," Mom said. "So if you didn't put it there, who did?"

"I don't know," I said looking around frantically. I looked up at the sweetheart apple tree. "There!" I pointed up at a part of the tree. Everyone else looked up. There was one spot where it looked like a branch had broken off.

"See," I said. "The branch must have broken off and landed just right to lock them in. It wasn't me."

"Nice try," Mom said looking back at me. "But the tree is just out of reach. The only way it came off on its own and landed just right to lock them in is if a good wind blew it off and over."

"She's right," Doug said looking at the tree closely.

"There's something weird about that tree," I said. "We're having nothing but trouble from it."

An apple came flying from the tree and nearly hit Sunny.

"HEY!" I yelled. Without thinking it through I started climbing the tree.

"Gil!" Mom yelled. "Be careful!"

"You can't blame that one on him." Sunny said.

"Right behind you!" Doug said. I could hear him climbing the tree behind me. We got up into the branches and started looking around. Doug looked up above. "I don't see anyone."

"The wind didn't just blow it off." I said. Doug climbed a bit higher and sat on a branch looking around. He looked down at me and then his eyes went wide.

"Gil! Duck!" Doug yelled. Now here's the thing. I'm the practical joker in the family. Not Doug. Not Gary. Just me. I'm the one that plays jokes on people. So, when Doug says duck, I don't question it. I ducked just as something went flying over my head.

"OW!" yelled Sunny.

"Where'd it come from?" I said angrily. I was going to strangle whoever threw it.

"That's enough!" Mom yelled. "Both of you down here now!" A look at Doug told me that he was ready to be out of the tree and I should be too. We shimmied down the tree and landed on the ground.

"What was it?" I asked Doug.

"The tree!" Doug said. His whole body was shaking. "That apple was on the tree and then suddenly it came loose from the branch. It nearly hit Gil!"

"Don't be stupid." Mom said.

"You're seriously calling me stupid?" Doug asked.

"No," Mom said. "Of course not, but it couldn't have come loose on its own."

"Mom," Doug said. "I'm telling you that's exactly what happened."

"Enough!" Mom said. "I've had enough from both of you."

"But Mom," I started.

"No buts!" Mom snapped. "I don't know what's gotten into the two of you, but I'm over it! Go! Just go. Wall duty in the dining room!"

"For how long?" I asked.

"Until I figure out what to do with the two of you!"

"Bianca," Uncle Hunter started.

"No!" Mom snapped at him. She waved a hand to include Dad. "I don't want to hear another word. I need to get Sunny to his doctor appointment."

# 11

Doug and I spent the rest of the week with wall duty. The only time we were allowed outside was to either paint the chicken coop or in the garden and only if one of the adults was with us the whole time.

The apple tree continued to assault our brothers at random, and Doug and I continued to get blamed despite the fact that with the constant supervision and insistence from Dad, Grandma and Uncle Hunter that we were never out of sight in order to do anything other than what we were assigned to do.

Doug was taking the false accusations much more personally, and honestly, I couldn't blame him. He'd always been the golden child of the family. I could almost appreciate Gary's resentment for Doug's status in the family.

"You two keep it up, and the house won't need the deep winter cleaning." Mom joked the day before we were to get registered in our new schools.

"Yeah," I agreed. "Too bad you're punishing us for stuff we're not doing."

"Don't start, Gil," Mom warned. "I don't know how you're manipulating that tree, but that tree isn't throwing apples all on its own. What I don't get is why Doug's going along with it."

"I saw what I saw," Doug said. "I can't help it that my own mother has gone mad and thinks we're suddenly turning into punks."

"I don't know what game you two think you're playing," Mom said in a tight voice. "But it needs to stop. And until it does, you two will keep up the work."

"You've been here this whole time watching us right?" I asked.

"Yes," Mom said sounding tired.

"And we haven't been anywhere but right here, right?"

"Yes," Mom said. Now she was getting irritated. I should have stopped there, but like Doug, I was tired of the accusations.

"So how do you explain this then?" I said

picking up an apple from the ground and holding up to her. "We sure didn't put it here, and it takes about five minutes to get to the apple tree."

"Can't blame that one on us," Doug said. "But of course, you'll figure out a way to do so, even though we've been here the whole time." Mom snatched the apple from my hand and marched away quickly.

"Wonder what she'll come up with this time?" I asked watching her storm off.

"You sound amused." Doug said bending back to his weeding.

"Take yourself out of the situation and it sort of is." I said. "You have to admire the level of creativity she has to go to in order to pin every instance on us." I turned back to Doug "What are we going to do? We can't keep going on like this. If we don't figure out what's going on with that apple tree, we'll be grounded forever and eventually she'll do worse than just making us clean."

"I don't know," Doug said standing back up and looking over to where the apple tree stood. We couldn't see it from where we stood, but it almost seemed to have its own presence. "Mom won't let us near it, but I agree with you. We have to get close enough to it to examine it.

There's something weird about that tree."

"You don't think Mom will really cancel the winter cleaning do you?" I asked giving him a nervous glance.

"Nah," Doug said going back to the weeding. "It's not her style. Why? You're not actually looking forward to it are you?"

"It just wouldn't seem right," I said. "The whole point of it is to make the house as comfortable as possible before locking ourselves in from the winter."

"Lots of people go into the winter without a winter cleaning and survive just fine." Doug said.

"Sure, they're surviving," I said. "But how comfortable are they? They lock themselves into some sort of winter prison with the plastic on the widows and all the rest instead of turning into something cozy and safe."

"Are you sure you're not enjoying the cleaning?" Doug said chuckling.

"I can't wait for school to start," I said with a sigh. "At least then I can get away from Mom and her insanity."

"Don't say that too loud," Doug muttered. "She's already upset with you."

"Good," I said bending back to the weeding. "At least then I'll get in trouble for something I actually did. You can't tell me you're not looking forward to the start of school too."

"Yeah," Doug agreed tossing some weeds into the wheelbarrow. "Maybe then Mom will remember that I'm actually the good and smart one."

"Alright," Mom said as she stormed back to us with the apple still in her hand. "How'd you do it?"

"Do what?" Doug asked annoyed.

"Get this apple to fall over here?" Mom said holding the apple out to us. Doug and I looked at each other in disbelief.

"You're seriously mental, you know that?" I snapped at her. I heard Doug suck in a breath. "You've been with us this entire time before that stupid apple appeared and you're still being so incredibly thick in the head that you think we had to have done it."

"There's no one else over there, Gil," Mom started.

"Including us!" I yelled cutting her off. I could see the gears working in Mom's head. On the one hand she really wanted to tell me off for yelling at her, but the logic of what I'd just said seemed to be taking hold too.

"Well," Mom said finally, "How else do you explain it then?"

"I don't know," I said finally. "Maybe it's possessed or something." Mom looked at me for a moment and then looked down at the apple in her hand.

"It is an old house," Mom mused finally.

"Seriously?" Doug asked. "Since when do you believe in ghosts?"

"I don't, of course," Mom said. "But it does give me an idea. I need to check something. You two keep working, and don't forget to put those in the compost."

"You're actually going to leave us here on our own?" I asked surprised. Mom didn't answer and continued up to the house.

"That was odd." Doug said. We finished our weeding and took the wheelbarrow to the compost pile and tossed the weeds onto the top of it.

"Let's go check on that tree." Doug said.

"We'll be in trouble for sure." I said. But I hurried to catch up to him.

"The warden isn't looking, and we may not have another chance to look at it." Doug said.

I looked around the trunk of the tree. The only thing that stood out was the engraving of the sweetheart's initials. LB + MD.

"Do you think that one of these people are haunting the tree?" I asked Doug. Doug came around and looked at the initials.

"Hard to tell," Doug said. "If they got married and raised kids, then probably not."

"What if they didn't get married?" I asked. "What if they didn't have the chance for some reason? Like what if their parents didn't approve?"

"I don't know," Doug said slowly. "Maybe if they disapproved their relationship, they might have chopped this tree down, or at least cut the initials out."

"If it was a working orchard, I don't think they'd waste a tree just because of the initials. Would cutting the out the initials hurt the tree at all?" I asked.

"I don't know," Doug said again. "Looks like we have our own research to do."

# 12

The Tawny Delis Middle School was nothing special. It was a three-story red brick building with a flat roof. It looked like many of the other schools we'd attended. A large statue of a chicken, or maybe it was a rooster greeted us as we walked into the building.

"What in the world is that?" I asked.

"I think it's the school mascot." Mom said.

"Uh, I think we'll wait in the car." Doug said exchanging looks with Gary. The two of them turned and went back to the van.

"Can Dennis and I wait in the van too?" Sylvester asked.

"Sure," Mom said handing him the keys.

"Go Mighty Clucks!" Gary shouted from the van causing Doug and Sylvester to laugh.

"Don't worry," Mom said. "Usually whatever the mascot for the middle school is transfers to the high school."

"Oh, please let Gary and Doug play a sport this year." I prayed out loud.

"I will definitely show up to their games and cheer them on with the chicken dance." Baxter laughed.

There were two other boys waiting in the office when we arrived. One had sandy brown hair, sun-tanned skin, large round ears, and an angular face. He was wearing a blue shirt and tan pants. The other had dark brown hair, black beadlike eyes, and fair skin. His favorite color was probably dark brown judging from the dark brown shirt and jeans he was wearing. They were both thin but the boy in blue was shorter than the other boy. The boy in brown looked like he was waiting for his body to grow into his long legs and arms.

"Are you boys starting at this school too?" a woman behind the receptionist's desk asked. She had jet black hair pulled into two tight buns on her head in the pigtail position. Her pink high heel shoes matched the pink dress with white polka dots. She kind of reminded me of a teacher I'd had in kindergarten.

"Yes, they are," Mom answered. "Are you the administrator?"

"I'm the principal," the woman said. "The admin staff are still on vacation. The guidance Counselor and I are just here to get the new students enrolled. I'm Principal Wilhelmina Mowse. Everyone calls me Mina though. Principal Mina to the students."

"Don't principals and teachers usually go by their last name? I asked.

"Yes," Principal Mina said with a laugh. "As long as their last name doesn't sound like a rodent. My last name is spelled M-O-W-S-E. But it's pronounced Mouse, so I just go by Mina."

"Any relation to Mayor Mowse?" Mom asked.

"As a matter of fact, yes," Principal Mina laughed. "Michael is my husband."

"Small world." Mom said with a smile.

"More like small town," Principal said. "Tawny Delis isn't that big."

"Well, is it alright to just leave them here?" Mom asked nodding her head at Baxter, Sunny and me. "I have their paperwork here, but I need to get to the high school and elementary school to get my other sons enrolled."

"Yeah," Principal Mina said and waved a

hand at the other two boys sitting in the office. "These two were dropped off with their paperwork too. You can pick them back up at half past one unless they know the way home from here."

"We do." I answered quickly.

"You're sure?" Mom asked. "I can pick you up after I get Sylvester and Dennis registered."

"We're going to have to walk to and from school anyway," Sunny said. "And we don't live too far."

"Alright," Mom said giving us a final look. "Be good. I don't want to hear about you guys having detention before school even starts."

"I'm sure they'll be fine." Principal Mina said.

Mom handed the papers over to Principal Mina and hesitated before going on. "My son, Sunny was on some medications. The doctor has taken him off of them for now, but he may end up back on most of them again…"

"Alright," Principal Mina said looking through the papers. "If he does and he has any that need to be administered during the school day, you can bring the prescription to the school and give them to the nurse with instructions and we can take it from there."

"Be good." Mom said again before leaving

us to the principal.

"I'll just take these into the guidance counselor," Principal Mina said getting to her feet. "You boys just wait here." She left the room and went down a hall leading off of the main office.

"My name's Joey Jeroho." the sandy haired boy in the blue shirt said. "This is my best friend Harold Packard."

"Nice to meet you," I said shaking Joey's hand. "I'm Gil Blanc. This is my twin brother Baxter, and our little brother Sunny. He's starting the sixth grade this year. Baxter and I are in the seventh."

"We're in the seventh grade too," Joey said. "Where do you live?"

"In the house with all the apple trees." Sunny said.

"Isn't one of those apple trees cursed?" Harold asked. We all looked at him in shock.

"Guess you hadn't heard," Joey said. "Tawny Delis is cursed. Harold and I moved here after the end of the school year this summer."

"We moved in a week ago," I said. "What do you mean Tawny Delis is cursed?"

"The guy that founded the town, Tawny Delis. The town was named after him." Joey said. "He built his house and started the town and everything. Then the Mowse family moved in and suddenly the townspeople liked them better, so they voted for all the Mowse family members to offices like the school board, Mayor, and whatnot. Tawny thought it was an injustice and cursed the whole town until the injustice was resolved, but now every time there's an injustice, the curse activates, and you can't just undo the whole curse. You have to take them on one by one."

"So how do we uncurse our apple tree?" I asked. "Because it's definitely cursed and I'm getting in trouble for it."

"You mean that apple tree really is throwing apples at people?" Sunny asked his eyes going wide.

"I really thought you were making that up." Baxter said.

"We had something happen like that at the boarding house," Joey said. "I found a cookbook that Tawny Delis himself wrote, and everything I made from it came to life and made a mess."

"It was a real nightmare," Harold said with a shudder. "I still wake up in the night thinking those brownies are going to eat me."

"Seriously?" I asked. Joey and Harold both

nodded.

"So how do we break the curse?" Sunny asked. "Gil will be grounded forever if we can't get the tree to stop."

"Have you tried talking to it?" Harold asked.

"What do you know about the history of the property?" Joey asked.

"Nothing," I answered. "It's a sweetheart tree. There are initials carved into it. That's all we know so far."

"We can ask Principal Mina when she comes back out," Joey said. "She's a descendant of the Mowse family. She might know something about the property."

"Mom is never going to believe this." Sunny said sitting down in one of the chairs.

"So we don't tell her," I said taking a seat myself. "Besides, I'll only get into more trouble if she thinks I'm telling tales at school before the school year has even started."

"I agree," Baxter said leaning against the wall. "Let's wait and see if we can break the curse and then she'll just eventually lay off him when the attacks stop."

"Okay boys, you can come back to the office," Principal Mina said. "If you all will just follow me." We followed her down the hall.

"Do you know anything about the house we

live in?" I asked her as we walked along the hallway. "It's a large three-story house with an apple orchard."

"You must be in the old Ballard Place," Principal Mina said. "Yes, I know about it."

"The old Ballard Place?" a man asked as we entered an office. "Someone actually bought that place?" He was a tall thin man with large blue rimmed glasses, rosy cheeks, and a large red nose. He was bald on the top of his head, but loads of shaggy white hair stuck out from the sides of his head and cascaded down to the beard on his chin. He wore a grey blazer over a white polo shirt and gray slacks. He smiled broadly and I found that I liked him right away.

"My family did," I said. "Why is it called the Old Ballard Place?"

"Old man Ballard lived there," the man said. "I'm Mr. Aldwin. I'm one of the guidance counselors. I'll be getting you guys signed up for your classes."

"What do you know about Mr. Ballard?" I asked.

"Only that he's dead," Mr. Aldwin said. "Left everything to his daughter, Charlotte. She married Gabe Richards and had, what was it, like five kids? Yeah. Anyway, her kids put the place up for sale since they had no desire to maintain the place. It's just too big for any of them."

"Well, that gives us something to go on anyway." Sunny said.

"I'm glad you like history so much," Mr. Aldwin said looking over our school records. "You'll need history credits, all of you. Looks like you guys have been through a lot of different schools. Army Brats?"

"Yes." We all answered together.

"You're Army brats too?" I asked Joey and Harold.

"Yeah," Joey answered. He jerked a thumb at Harold. "We actually grew up together. Our dads get stationed in the same places a lot, so we got to be best friends."

"Lucky," Sunny asked. "Our dad is finally retired from the Army so this is the first chance we'll actually have to get to make any lasting friends."

"Alright, so American History for Sunny," Mr. Aldwin said typing something into his computer. "And for you four, we'll put you into the World History Class. It seems like you've had enough American History."

"I can recite the Declaration of Independence for you," I offered. "Or the Constitution or the Emancipation Proclamation."

"That's quite alright," Mr. Aldwin chuckled. "Looks like you've all done well in most of your math classes. Joseph, you and Harold haven't had Algebra yet?"

"It's Joey, and no." Joey answered.

"You two have," Mr. Aldwin glanced at Baxter and I. "Algebra two then for you I think."

"It looks like you've had all the science we offer, but you're still lacking science credits for going on to High school."

"Biology!" Baxter said quickly.

"Yeah, we don't mind more biology." I agreed.

"It says here you've had it for the last three years." Mr. Aldwin said looking at our transcripts.

"We were able to take a biology class in our fifth year as part of the advanced science class," I explained. "But every biology class we've taken has been different, so we'll probably actually learn something new in this one."

"Works for me," Mr. Aldwin said. "You'll need to choose two electives and one foreign language class." He pushed two pieces of paper towards us across the desk. One had a list of languages offered and one was a list of electives.

"Spanish." Joey and Harold both said at once. I glanced at the language paper and pushed it aside. The five of us bent over the electives paper.

"You have sword fighting classes here?" Sunny asked.

"We do," Mr. Alden said smiling. "You won't start off with swords right away of course, but eventually you'll work your way up to it. That one you can take for your entire middle school career."

"Yes please!" Joey said excitedly. The rest of us nodded enthusiastically.

"Drama for me." I said pushing the paper over to the others.

"Oh, they have a herbology class here." Sunny said.

"I think I'd prefer debate team." Baxter said quietly. Sunny and I both stared at him.

"Something wrong?" Mr. Aldwin asked looking between us and Baxter.

"You?" I asked. "The guy who can barely squeak out a sound when meeting anybody. You are going to take debate?" Baxter just shrugged and looked down at his feet.

"Are you serious, Baxter?" Sunny asked. Baxter only nodded but didn't look up. I broke into a wide grin.

"Baxter, that's great!" I said. "I'm proud of you."

"Yeah," Sunny agreed. "Really cool." Baxter kept his head down, but he glanced up at us and smiled a small smile.

"I think you'll do just fine." Mr. Aldwin said.

"Home Economics for me," Joey said. "Harold."

"I kind of want to do herbology." Harold said shrugging at Joey. I got the feeling the two of them usually took all their classes together if they could help it.

"Cool," Joey said. "Your herbs will work great in my cooking."

"You three still need to choose a language." Mr. Aldwin said pushing the language paper back over to my brothers and me. I looked down at the paper helplessly.

"Nosotros hablamos espanol." I said. "Wir Sprechen Deutsh. On Parle Fransais."

"You all speak these three languages fluently?" Mr. Aldwin asked. The three of us nodded.

"We also speak Portugues fluently." Baxter said.

"Hazards of the upbringing," Joey said. "That's why we chose Spanish. It's the only one we don't speak fluently."

"You do speak it though?" Mr. Aldwin asked.

"We can speak it conversationally," Harold said. "Like enough to order food and to ask for directions."

"I am here," A man said popping his head into the office. "Mina is here?" He had a strange accent.

"Oleg," Principal Mina said with a bright smile. "Great. I need your help getting the classrooms organized so that the teachers can get their classes set up. They're coming in sometime this afternoon."

"Right," Mr. Aldwin said. "We're almost done here. So, if you boys can test out of all three classes we'll call it good. We can't really give you the credit if we don't have the test scores to back it up."

"So, we just pass the final exam on each one and that's it?" Sunny asked.

"What languages do you speak?" I asked Oleg.

"I speak English okay," Oleg said. "I speak Russian best."

"Russian is his first language." Principal Mina said.

"I wish I could take Russian." I muttered.

"I think we could clear an hour of Oleg's

cleaning schedule to allow him to teach you Russian if you're both willing."

"I can teach Russian." Oleg said in halting English. "But after school. I need to be in school for unexpected things."

"I don't mind staying an hour after school each day." I said.

"Well, that settles it, then," Mr. Aldwin said. "I'll put you down for uh....hmm how to do this...Ah here we go. We'll just do it this way." He typed something into the computer and then hit a button with a flourish. The printer started spitting out papers. Mr. Aldwin jumped up and grabbed them and after leafing through them quickly, handed them out to each of us. Our class schedule for the school year.

"Hey!" I said looking at my paper. "Detention?" Sunny and Baxter looked over my shoulder at my paper.

"It's the only way I could get the computer to accept a class for you for an hour after the end of the school day." Mr. Aldwin said. "I'll talk to the I.T. guy and see if we can't get it fixed so that it doesn't stay on your permanent record."

"Mom's going to kill you." Sunny laughed.

"One more thing," Mr. Aldwin said. "Every student is required to serve in some way in the community to advance to the next grade. It's the school's way to encourage community involvement in our students."

"Sounds more like it's forced than encouraged." I said.

"There's a table outside the office with different ways to serve and we'll be holding an assembly the third week of school in the gymnasium."

"Okay," Principal Mina said. "I think that's it. Any questions?"

"Just one," I said. "Why is our mascot a chicken?"

# 13

"Only you could talk your way *into* detention." Mom said shaking her head and looking down at my class schedule.

"But I didn't do anything wrong this time." I pointed out.

"I know," Mom said handing it back to me. "And honestly, I don't know why I'm surprised because of all of my kids, you're definitely the one that would have after school detention every day for the whole school year for a decent reason."

"Hey!" Doug said. "I thought I was your good kid."

"You are," Mom said. "You're so good, that you wouldn't get detention for any reason at all. Gil is my Chaotic Good kid."

"Good intentions, but questionable methods." Gary chuckled. "So, what does that make me?"

"My sourpuss." Mom said turning back to the stove. She was making us spaghetti for lunch with garlic bread and a salad. Dennis was making the salad.

"So, which of you are going to be the school mascot?" Uncle Hunter asked.

"Neither of us." Sunny said wrinkling his nose.

"They're mascot is a chicken." Laughed Doug.

"What's the high school mascot?" I asked.

"A bulldog." Gary answered.

"We're salamanders," Sylvester said with a grimace. "I still think it's better than chickens, but I'm not looking forward to middle school."

"We're actually Roosters," I told them. "Principal Mina said the school originally didn't have a mascot, so they allowed the students to pick the animal.

"They chose a rooster because there's a rooster named Douglas that thinks the school is his home. The staff had been trying to get it to relocate, but the kids liked him, so they figured if they made their mascot a rooster, he'd be allowed to stay. It worked because he has his own little house in the courtyard of the school, and they even gave him some hens."

"The same thing happened at the elementary school." Baxter said. "Principal Mina said everyone thought the kids would either choose the bulldogs like the high school, or something along the lines of a mouse or a rat since the Mowse family is so prominent here."

"How did the elementary school kids come up with a salamander?" Sylvester asked.

"Most of the teachers have salamanders as a class pet," Baxter answered. "So, the students wanted to make sure they were included since they felt it was the salamander's school too."

"Also, we have to volunteer somewhere in the community." Doug said.

"So do we," I said pulling a pamphlet out of my pocket. "They had some options already laid out on a table by the office and I chose this one."

"A nursing home?" Mom asked glancing at the pamphlet in my hand.

"Yeah," I said. "I thought I should start looking for a good place to put you when you're older."

"That's not nice." Mom snapped.

"Can you blame him?" Doug muttered. "You've been on him almost since we've moved in about something he hasn't done."

"Actually," I said. "I got some information about the house and the family that lived here before us. And I thought that volunteering for the nursing home would be a good place to get more information on the family."

"You could put some effort into our family history," Mom said. "Your father and I can both trace our family lines back to royalty."

"Your family isn't cursing a tree that keeps getting me into trouble." I said. Mom started laughing.

"You think the tree is cursed?" Mom asked.

"How else do you explain it?" I asked. "I'm adamant that I'm not throwing apples, you insist that apple trees can't throw their own apples, and you're right. Normal trees can't throw apples."

"And that apple tree is the only one that had red apples on it in the whole orchard." Doug said.

"We're going to need to get them harvested soon." Mom said. I looked at Doug. Mom seemed to be avoiding the whole apple throwing subject and she wasn't getting upset like she had been.

"I think some of the older folks in the nursing home might know about Charlotte

Ballard," I continued. "She was the only daughter of the man that lived here, and she had five kids. Maybe one of them put the initials on that tree."

"What initials?" Mom asked. Doug, Sunny, and I told her about the initials we'd seen on the tree.

"Show me after lunch," Mom said pulling the garlic bread out of the oven. "Dad and Grandma are out shopping for flowers so it's just us and Uncle Hunter."

"Should we save them some?" Uncle Hunter asked.

"Ian said they'd grab something while they were out." Mom said. The nine of us dug into our lunch and talked about the different ways we'd serve in the community for school. The apple tree wasn't mentioned again until after we'd cleaned up when Mom reminded us that she wanted us to show her the initials.

"See?" I said pointing to the initials. "It's a sweetheart tree."

"It is indeed," Mom said. "But these wouldn't be any of her children's initials. Their last name was Richards. It might be Charlotte's father's initials here since his last name was Ballard." She pointed a finger at the LB. The tree started to shudder. Doug, Sunny, and I instinctively covered our heads as a few apples rained down on us. Mom looked up into the branches.

"Do you see anyone?" Uncle Hunter asked.

"No," Mom said. "I don't think it's a someone. I'm starting to think it's a something." My brothers and I looked up into the branches too. Dennis was about to climb up when Mom shot out a hand and stopped him.

"No one is to climb this tree right now," Mom said. "I don't want to see any of you up there, understand?" We all nodded.

"You don't really think it's cursed do you?" Uncle Hunter asked.

"No," Mom said leading us back to the house. "But something might be living in that tree, and I don't want anyone getting near it."

"Does that mean you actually believe us then?" Doug asked. "That Gil and I aren't attacking our little brothers?"

"I never thought you were attacking them." Mom said. "I thought Gil was playing one of his pranks and acting out because of your father leaving the Army."

"Wait, what?" I asked stopping short.

"You were upset about your father not being in the Army anymore," Mom said. "You didn't really say anything, but we could tell it was bothering you."

"You haven't been your cheerful self lately." Doug said. "You've seemed kind of, I don't know, depressed I guess?"

"I mean, I'm going to miss traveling around and seeing different places, and I liked learning new languages," I said with a shrug. "I wasn't really upset about it; I just didn't know what it would mean for us to not be in the Army anymore."

"Well," Mom said looking around. "First of all, it means I won't feel like a single parent anymore. I still don't know what's going on with that tree, so I won't apologize just yet. But I'll let you off the hook for now. I'm still going to be keeping a close eye on you though."

"It's a start." I said throwing my hands in the air with a sigh. I couldn't really expect much more than that from Mom. She was the kind of person that never admitted to anything if she couldn't be sure about it. And honestly, seeing things from her point of view, I could see why she was still so suspicious.

# 14

I had just finished my breakfast the following morning when I heard a knock on the door. I went to answer it since the rest of my family were all still eating.

"Good morning," Joey Jeroho said when I opened the door. Harold was with him. "I hope we're not bothering you guys too early."

"Not at all," I said with a grin. "We're just finishing breakfast. Come on in." I led them through the house to the kitchen and introduced them to everyone.

"Of course, Gil's made new friends already." Dad chuckled.

"They're Army Brats too." Baxter said.

"Our dads are Army Rangers." Harold said.

"Pass," Dad said. "That's more than what

I'm cut out for."

"Have you ever tried?" I asked.

"Nope," Dad said. "Never really considered it either. I was happy being a drill sergeant."

"So, what are you boys up to today?" Mom asked getting up from the table and clearing the breakfast dishes away.

"We came to see the garden and chicken coop," Joey said. "Then we thought we'd ask Gil if he wanted to head over to the nursing home to sign up for the adopt a grandparent program for school."

"What?" Grandma asked in mock offense. "I'm not good enough for you?"

"I have to do some kind of volunteer service for school," I told her. "Besides, I never got to meet Grandpa."

"Don't bring home any brochures for that place," Mom said with a smile. "Unless the orderlies are handsome young men."

"Or pretty nurses." Uncle Hunter added.

I led Harold and Joey out to the garden and pointed out what we had planted and what was nearly ready to be harvested. Then we walked over to the chicken coop which was still too close to the orchard for my comfort.

"We're getting the chicks next spring," I

said. "The apple tree is over here." Harold, Joey and I walked around the tree and stopped to look at the initials carved into the tree.

"Don't these things usually have like a heart around them or something?" Joey asked. "How do we know they were sweethearts and not just best friends?"

"The initials aren't really that big," I said. "If they were trying to hide the fact that they were sweethearts, then a heart would have been a dead giveaway. I think they just carved their initials here, so they knew which tree to meet at or leave things for each other. Big enough for them to see since they knew what they were looking for, but small enough that it wouldn't be very noticeable."

"Makes sense," Joey nodded looking up into the tree branches. Harold turned away from the tree and looked at the other trees.

"I don't get it," Harold said. "What makes this tree different from all of these other trees? It looks just like all the others." An apple flew from the tree and hit Harold in the head. Harold whirled around to face me. "What'd you do that for?" Harold asked rubbing his head.

"He didn't," Joey said his eyes wide. "The tree did. I just saw it."

"You did?" I asked looking up into the tree.

"Doug said he'd seen it do it once too, but I've never seen it do it. I just know the apples are coming from this tree."

"This tree is definitely cursed," Joey said. "There's been an injustice done here for sure. We need to figure out what it is and sort it out before the tree causes real harm to someone."

"Try talking to it." Harold suggested.

"Um okay..." I said doubtfully.

"Hi tree...er...are you having a good day today?" The apple tree didn't move. "Are you mad at me?" The tree remained still. "Are you mad at my family for moving here?" The tree stayed still, and I was starting to feel stupid.

"Maybe you're asking it the wrong questions." Harold said.

"Well, I'm not used to talking to trees," I told him. "I'm not sure what I'm supposed to say or ask it."

"Let's go to the nursing home," Joey suggested. "The sooner we get signed up, the better."

Joey was right about the nursing home. The lady at the front desk sent us into a waiting room. We had to wait until the coordinator was done with helping the residents get their breakfasts before we could sign up. We signed our names on the volunteer roster and took our seats. We'd only just sat down when three more kids showed up to sign in. Before long, the room was full of kids who had come to sign up for the adopt-a-grandparent program.

"Ah, looks like we have a nice group of volunteers this year," A woman said as she entered the room and picked up the sign-up sheet. "Gil Blanc?" I raised my hand. "First to arrive, first to pick."

"Pick?" I asked as she handed me a clip board.

"Your grandparent," the woman explained pointing to the clipboard in my hand. "That's a list of all the residences that are interested in an adopted grandchild. Just pick a name on the list and that's who we'll pair you with. Pass it to your left and I'll introduce myself and explain more about the program."

"Oh, okay." I said. I scanned the names. I was about to choose a male name at random when one of the grandmother's names jumped out at me. Charlotte Richards. The daughter of the man that owned the apple orchard was here at the nursing home.

I was shocked at first, then I was kind of mad. Five kids. The woman had five kids and not only had they sold her childhood home, but they stuck her in a nursing home. Not a single one of them had been willing to take her into their own home and care for her. I had joked with Mom that I was going to put her in a home, but it was just that. A joke. The reality of the situation was that either Dennis or I would end up caring for Mom and Dad in their old age.

I put my name next to Charlotte's name. It wasn't just curiosity that made me do it. I was living in her childhood home and her kids had left her here. I felt kind of responsible for her. I had to be the grandkid none of her real grandkids could be.

"My name is Kendra Knight. I'm the activities coordinator here at the nursing home." The woman said.

For the next ten minutes Kendra told us about the rules for being in the program and that we were expected to come to certain activities to spend time with our grandparents. She also told us that we were welcome to come visit them as often as we'd like as long as it was okay with our parents and during visiting hours. We were given a paper with the rules, the activity schedule and the visiting hours. Then we were taken on a tour of the facility.

We were shown where to sign in each time we came to visit. The dining room, the community center, and the physical therapy center before being taken into the activity room where several old people were sitting in chairs or wheelchairs. There was a man sitting at table with checkers laid out. A woman at another table was working on a puzzle. One man sat by the window in his wheelchair knitting something. They all stopped what they were doing when we walked in.

"These are the grandparents you've adopted," Kendra said waving a hand to include the room full of old folks. Kendra looked down at the clipboard. "We're going to let you all sit a bit with your grandparents and get to know them a bit better. Gil, this lovely lady is your grandmother Charlotte." Kendra gestured to the woman sitting at the puzzle table. I smiled and walked over and sat down next to her. She was a very thin old woman with curly white hair, round glasses and a big smile.

"Hi," I said. "I'm Gil Blanc. Are you Charlotte Richards?"

"I am," The woman said. "Do you like puzzles?"

"I love them." I said looking down at the jigsaw puzzle. It was true. Jigsaw puzzles was Baxter and my favorite way to pass time on a rainy day.

"So what grade are you in?" Mrs. Richards asked.

"Seventh," I answered. "My family just moved here this summer. I think we're living in your old house."

"The three-story house with the apple orchard?" Mrs. Richards asked.

"That's the one," I said. "We built a chicken coop so that we can have chickens and we have an herb garden and a vegetable garden, and my brother Sylvester is making a place for the family to gather around the fire pit."

"That all sounds wonderful!" Mrs. Richards exclaimed clapping her hands together. "I'm so glad a family has moved into it and is making it a home. I did love growing up there so much."

"Why did your kids sell it Mrs. Richards?" Didn't they like growing up there?"

"Oh yes! And call me Lottie. Everyone does." She answered. "My three boys used to play in the woods out behind the orchard. That's part of your property too you know."

"I did know." I told her.

"Well, if you go back in those woods a bit, I'll bet you'll find their clubhouse they built back there."

"They built a clubhouse?" I asked in amazement. I had actually thought of checking out the woods for that very purpose. Knowing there was one back there already was good information to have.

"Oh yes." Lottie said. "The girls weren't allowed back there, but they didn't mind. They spent most of their time in the Apple barn. Who knows what treasures you'll find in there from their younger days."

"So why did they sell it?" I asked.

"It's too big for my eldest son, Jamie" Lottie explained. "He hasn't married, and I don't know if he ever will. He travels a lot for work and is perfectly fine living in his camper. My second eldest, my daughter Barb married a man who took a job in Texas. No since having a house in Massachusetts for them.

"My son Shayne hates the cold and moved to Alabama. He owns some condos down there. Theodore lives in Germany with his wife and kids. And Shirley is the only one who lives here in town. She's the one who took on the job of selling the house. She would have loved to have kept it, but she just couldn't manage such a large place on her own and my other kids never come to visit.

"She insisted that the estate had to be sold intact and could not be parceled out. She also wanted a family that would actually live there to take it on. She turned down many offers for the place from people who had no intention of living there and just wanted to tear everything down and sell off the land in pieces or turn it into some new development. She told me that she sold it for much less than the market says it's worth simply because the family was the first to actually want it. I understand you have a big family too."

"Yes Ma'am," I answered. "There're my parents. My six brothers, my uncle, and my grandmother."

"If you already have a grandmother, why did you choose to adopt another one?"

"I was hoping people here could tell me the history of the house and the town."

"Oh, a history buff are you?" Lottie chuckled. "Well, you certainly picked the right grandmother then. My family has been here since Old Tawny Delis himself cursed the town. I can tell you stories many others can't."

"Awesome." I breathed.

# 15

Lottie wasn't able to tell me any stories while we were getting to know each other because she wanted to know more about the things my family was doing to make the place our own.

I was just about to ask her if she knew who the sweetheart's initials carved into the tree was when Kendra announced that it was time for us to leave.

"I have so many more questions." I told Lottie.

"You can ask me some more questions next time."

"When is next time?"

"Why don't you come after you're out of your first day of school?" Lottie said. "You can tell me all about your first day, and I can tell you all about my childhood growing up in the apple orchard."

"It's a deal." I said. I gave her a hug and said goodbye.

"My grandfather used to be a pilot," Joey said. "He's been all over the world."

"Mine used to be a radio D.J." Harold said. "He's funny."

"My grandmother used to live in the house my family lives in now." I said. All the way back to my house I told them everything that Lottie Richard's had told me about the house and the clubhouse hidden somewhere in the woods.

"Are you going to tell your brothers about it?" Joey asked.

"Are you kidding?" I asked. "For once I have something that's just mine. At least for now. No. No way am I going to tell them about it."

"They'll eventually find it though, won't they?" asked Harold.

"Maybe," I said. "But as far as I know, they haven't found it yet. So, I'll just have to find it first and claim it for ourselves. They can't fault me if I claim it first right?"

"How should we know?" Joey said. "I'm an only child. Harold is the closest thing to a brother I've ever had and he's an only child too."

"I wonder what that's like?" I mused out loud. "No one to share your bedroom with, and no one to blame stuff on you when things go wrong."

"No one to play with on rainy days when your friends are all stuck in their homes." Joey muttered.

"No one to tell secrets too that you can't tell your parents." Harold added.

"I sometimes wish I had a brother or two," Joey said. "But I can't imagine having six brothers. I don't think I'd want that many."

"Yeah, seems like a lot of brothers." Harold agreed.

"It's not like I chose to have so many brothers." I told them as we reached the apple orchard. I pointed towards the woods just behind the sweetheart's tree. "There's where the woods start. Let's go."

"If you had to choose, which of your brothers would you give up?" Harold asked as we entered the woods. The trees in the apple orchard were spread far apart, but the trees here in the woods grew close together creating a shady canopy above us that made the air in the woods dark and cool. There was a path that wound it's way into the woods. I suppose Mrs. Richard's sons had created it.

"Which brother would I choose to give up?" I repeated as we followed the path. "I'm not sure. Doug's pretty smart, and if he weren't around I would have had to figure out how to build the chicken coop and plant the garden all on my own. Baxter is my twin brother, and I can't imagine him not being here. Gary is kind of grumpy most of the time…I don't know. I'd have to think about that one."

We followed the path winding its way through the woods for about ten minutes before we found it. I don't know what I expected. Probably just a little hut type of thing sitting on the ground surrounded by some trees or something. The clubhouse wasn't on the ground at all. It was a tree house. There was an old rope ladder hanging from the platform that was supported by four trees.

A faded gray tarp had been stretched over the roof and was secured with what looked like string. A squirrel sat on the rail that wrapped around the platform looking down at us like a sentry looking out for potential intruders. Joey, Harold and I all looked at each other smiles spreading across our faces.

I grabbed a hold of the rope ladder and started climbing up. Or at least I tried to climb up. The first rope rung held my weight, but the second one snapped as soon as I put my full weight on it. I stumbled forward and then back and was nearly tangled in the rope as the top of it came loose from the platform and tumbled heavy and wet around me.

"Are you alright?" Joey asked as he and Harold helped get me free of the rope mess.

"I'm fine," I coughed. "Come on. Gary might have a ladder in his apple barn."

Gary was in the apple barn banging on a piece of wood with a hammer. There was light pouring in through the windows making the whole area visible.

"Woah," I said when I entered. "Cool space."

"Thanks," Gary muttered. "What'd you want?"

"I've never seen a barn shaped like this before." Joey said looking around. It was an octagonal shaped building and no stalls or anything you'd normally see in a regular barn.

"It's an apple barn," Gary said as if that explained everything. "What do you want?"

"Do you have a ladder we can use?" I asked.

"For how long?"

"Uh...for a while?" I asked.

"Like for a few hours, or a few days or?" Gary asked.

"Probably a few days." I said. Gary stood up and looked at me for a moment.

"What do you need it for?" Gary asked. I looked at Joey and Harold.

"Uh, I can't say."

"You can't say to me, or you can't say to everyone else?"

"Everyone else." I answered.

"A secret project?" Gary asked his eyes lighting up. "Alright, I'm in. Let's go." He walked over to a wall with some ladders hanging on it and reached out to touch one. "This one big enough?"

"Yeah." I said. He pulled it down from the hook and tucking it under his arm and turned back to us.

"Alright, lead the way." Gary said. Joey and Harold hesitated.

"It's alright," I told them. "Gary won't tell anyone. Besides, he might have some ideas to help us." We led Gary out of the barn and into the woods to the treehouse. He whistled softly when he saw it.

"Sweet." Gary said. "How'd you find this?" I told him about Mrs. Richards and how her sons had built it.

"Let's get up there and check it out." Joey said.

"Not so fast," Gary said. "If the rope is rotting away, there's no telling how much more is rotting away, better let me go first and make sure it's safe."

"No fair!" I exclaimed. "We found it; we should go first."

"I'm the older brother," Gary said. "If you get hurt all I'm going to hear from Mom and Dad is 'Why didn't you go first?' and 'You're supposed to be watching out for him.' No way. I'm going first, and then you can come up when I know it's safe. You can take the lead on how you want it to be restored, but I'm not letting you fall through the floor and break your neck."

Gary leaned the ladder up where the rope ladder had once been and started climbing up. Once he got level with the platform he looked around at the boards and then climbed the rest of the way up. He took a few tentative steps forward and then walked all the way around it.

"The floor's in pretty good shape," he called down. "Come on up." Joey, Harold, and I scrambled up the ladder. Gary was looking into the door of the treehouse.

"Is it safe?" I asked. It smelled kind of musty

inside like a thick mossy blanket was hanging invisibly in the air. Gary took a gentle step inside causing the floorboards to creak and groan. Harold, Joey, and I held our breaths. Gary took another step in and bounced a bit. Soon he was walking gingerly all around the interior making slow strategic circles towards the center.

"The floor looks pretty solid," Gary said looking up at the ceiling. "Looks like they did a good job on the roof. I'd like to get the tarp off and see what's under it."

"I thought the roof was just the old gray tarp," Harold said looking up at the wooden beams.

"Nope," Gary said smiling. "They did better. The roof is wooden and then there's a tin sheet on top of that and then the tarp. I'm not sure what the purpose of the tarp was, but who knows how the people that built this thought when they were constructing it?"

"So how should we go about renovating it?" I asked.

"You won't have to do much," Gary said. "The railing outside looks like it might need replaced, and you might want a bucket and pully system so you can use both hands to climb up. And obviously a new ladder."

He pulled out his phone and started taking pictures. Now that we knew it was safe enough to walk around, we all started to examine the building carefully. It was a pretty sound structure all things considered. The frame of the roof was still pretty solid.

We untied the tarp and took it off. It was tattered and torn in places and really wasn't worth much, so we tossed it over the banister to take back up the house and dispose of properly. Under the tarp were two large, corrugated tin sheets that met at the apex of the roof. There was a small gap at the top which meant that the rain would have gotten under the tin sheets and had been trapped between the tin sheets and the wooden roof had it not been for the roof cap that had been placed on it. There were even some small gutters that had been made from PVC pipe that ran to a corner and down a hose to the ground.

The windows were covered in a thick plastic, but otherwise had nothing in them. If we wanted to hang out in here in the winter, some real windows would have to go in.

"Another trip to the hardware store," Gary said. "I think I can talk Dad into it."

"Okay," Joey said looking around. "A new ladder, rails, and maybe put some real windows in. Do we know anyone who can do that?"

"I think I can," Gary said. "I think a lot of this can be saved and what can't, should be easy enough to replace." He looked at his watch. "We need to get back to the house. Mom will be getting dinner ready."

"Is it that late already?" I asked. "I haven't even had lunch yet." My stomach growled in response.

"We'd better be getting home too then." Joey said.

"See you at school next week." Harold said as he and Joey started climbing down the ladder.

"Wait!" I said rushing out of the treehouse after them. "You're not coming back tomorrow?"

"Can't," Joey said. "Our parents are taking us back to school shopping and then we have to spend the rest of the week refreshing ourselves on school stuff."

"Our parents worry about the whole Summer amnesia thing where kids forget everything they learned the term before."

"Oh, okay," I said. "See you next Monday then." I leaned on the rail as I watched them disappear out of sight. A crack ripped through the air and suddenly there was nothing under me but air. Gary had been right. The railing definitely needed to be replaced.

# 16

By the time I registered what had happened I was lying on my back on the ground looking up into the trees. Suddenly, Gary's anxious face hovered over me.

"Are you alright?" Gary asked.

"I...I think so..." I groaned. I tried to sit up, but Gary pushed me back down.

"Don't move," Gary said. "You might be really hurt. Stay here until I get back." His face disappeared from view, and I could hear his tennis shoes pounding against the ground as he ran off. He was getting help. I groaned again and tried to yell out to him.

"Don't bring everyone!" I called out. It felt weak and croaky in my throat. What if he was right? What if I was badly hurt? I'd miss the first week of school. I'd miss my first Russian lessons. I'd miss out on being able to talk to Mrs. Richards again.

And what if he did end up bringing everyone? What if my brothers came and they saw the treehouse. I know it sounds selfish, but seriously. Nothing is ever just mine. I always have to share everything and just this once, I wanted something that was just mine. It wasn't just mine though, I realized. I was already sharing it with Gary. I had to. He was helping us rebuild it. It was only fair.

More foot pounding. Only the pounding was getting closer not farther. I tried to turn my head, but everything hurt.

"Gil," Uncle Hunter said. "Gil, are you alright? What happened?"

"He fell from up there," Gary said. I could see him pointing up at the tree house.

"I'm going to lift your head a bit," Uncle Hunter said. "Is that okay?"

"Yeah," I answered. "I…I think I'm okay, I just hurt everywhere." Uncle Hunter lifted my head and looked under it.

"Okay, good," Uncle Hunter said. "You don't seem to have hit your head on anything, and it's not bleeding. Lay still for a moment." He ran his hands carefully over my body. My arms, chest, hips and legs.

"Watch out for my ticklish spots." I joked.

"Very funny," Uncle Hunter said with a small smile. "Alright, you don't seem to have any broken bones. Take a deep breath for me and tell me how that feels."

"It feels like I took a deep breath." I said after doing what he asked. He asked me to wiggle my fingers and move my feet and I did.

"Good, I think you had a pretty good fall, but I think you're going to live. Let's get you back to the house. No, don't get up. I've got you." He scooped me up into his arms and started carrying me back to the house.

"We have to tell everyone he fell out of a tree." Gary said.

"Well, he did, didn't he?" Uncle Hunter said.

"He means we want to keep the treehouse a secret," I told him. "We don't want the others to know about it."

"A secret treehouse for the two of you huh?" Uncle Hunter chuckled.

"It's Gil's treehouse," Gary said. "I'm just helping him get it renovated so that he and his friends can be in it safely. It was built really well, and I think other than replacing the rails and a few boards here and there, it'll be fine."

"Your secret is safe with me." Uncle Hunter

said.

"GIL!" Mom exclaimed. I heard the kitchen's screen door slam as Mom came running out to us. "What happened? Is he alright? Gil, what happened?"

"He's fine, Bianca," Uncle Hunter said as Mom fussed over me. "Let me get him in the car and we can take him to the emergency room just in case."

"The emergency room?" Mom asked. "I'm coming with you. Gary, go tell your grandmother and your father what happened and help your grandmother with dinner."

"I'm on it." Gary said running into the house.

The emergency room was full of people. Uncle Hunter carried me in and up to the receptionist to explain the situation. The receptionist handed Mom a clipboard with paper attached to it and a pen.

"I can walk," I said feeling a little self-conscious. "Probably."

"You said he fell from a tree?" the receptionist asked.

"That's what his brother said happened." Uncle Hunter said.

"Do you know if he's broken anything?" the receptionist asked.

"He can move his feet and hands," Uncle Hunter said. "And it didn't feel like any of his bigger bones were broken."

"Are you feeling any pain?" the receptionist asked.

"Yeah," I said pointing to my nose. "This doesn't hurt."

"You can use one of these," the nurse said with a chuckle as she waved someone over to us. A young man with a red vest approached us with a wheelchair. "Just in case."

"Thanks," Uncle Hunter said gently placing me in the chair. "Okay?" he asked me.

"Yeah," I muttered feeling stupid. "Great. Thanks." Uncle Hunter wheeled me over to the waiting area with everyone else that was waiting to be seen. I wrinkled my nose as the smell of Disinfectant that filled the air settled around me.

There was one kid with shoulder length black hair who was wearing only a pair of red shorts with his hand wrapped in a bandage talking to a tall slender man with dark hair who I assumed was his father.

"I didn't even use that much lighter fluid." He said to him as he rolled his eyes and shook his head.

There was a girl in a brown dress with long

blond hair tied back in a ribbon with her finger wrapped up and a mouse in a cage next to her.

"He bit me," the girl said. "He likes yogurt so I put some on my finger and he thought the whole finger was his snack."

"I fell from a tree." I told her.

"My name is Cindy." The girl said.

"Gil. I just moved here."

"I've lived here my whole life."

"Is the town really haunted?"

"It really is. You've heard about it?"

"Yeah. One of my new friends told me about it. He just moved here too. He's already broken one of the curses."

"You must be talking about the Jeroho kid. Yeah I heard about the mess with the cookbook up at Robin Woods Estates."

"Everyone's heard about that," The boy with the red shorts said. "I'm Boris. This is my uncle Blake." He jabbed the thumb of his good hand at the dark-haired man next to him.

"How do you do?" the uncle said.

"This is my Uncle Hunter, and my mom, Bianca. What happened to you?"

"He tried to set his hand on fire." Blake answered.

"I didn't, Uncle Bernard did," Boris said. "I live with my two uncles. Uncle Bernard was teaching me how to make a fire."

"The laziest way possible, of course." Blake said.

"You must be Gil Blanc." A voice said. I looked up to see a woman in blue scrubs coming over to us.

"How'd you know?" I asked.

"I know all the kids in town," she said. "There isn't one that hasn't been in except you. You're new to town?"

"Yeah, I've got six brothers though, so you'll probably see them at some point."

"I doubt you could get Sylvester motivated to do anything ambitious enough to merit a visit here." Mom said rolling her eyes.

"You can come back now." The woman said. She led Mom and Uncle Hunter through a door and down a hall to a small cubicle with what passed as a bed or examining table. I'm not sure what they actually call them but it felt good to lay back and just rest for a moment. The disinfectant smell was stronger now that we were among the patients actually being attended to.

"Mrs. Blanc!" A man's voice exclaimed. A man stepped around the curtain that blocked the view of the cubicle from any passing people. He was pale, tall, and thin with a lot of bushy red hair. I could see a multi-colored shirt under his white lab coat. He smiled and cocked his head to the side when he saw me.

"So, I finally get to meet another Blanc boy eh?" he asked.

"Dr. Bugsy!" Mom exclaimed. "What are you doing here?"

"I got called in for one of my other patients that had to come in for an emergency situation. He'll be fine. What happened here? I was told he fell out of a tree? How did that happen?"

"I was climbing a tree with my older brother and a couple of friends," I said. "I was leaning against a…branch. And the next thing I know I was on the ground."

"I'm not surprised," Dr. Bugsy said his grin getting bigger. "We get a lot of kids injured around this time of year. Kids getting the last bit of summer in before the school year starts."

"Is your name really Bugsy?" I asked.

"Terrible joke of my father," Dr. Bugsy said. "Benjamin Siegel is one of my ancestors. You probably know him best as Bugsy."

"You mean the gangster?" I asked.

"The one and only," Dr. Bugsy said. "My surname is actually Siegel, but I prefer to go by Bugsy since most of my patients are children and it makes them laugh."

"Dr. Bugsy is one of our family doctors. Mom said. "You met his partner Dr. Harland when you got your vaccines."

"Oh yeah," I said. "The guy with the greyish brown hair and long ears."

"Gil!" Mom gasped. "That's not nice."

"It's also not wrong," Chuckled Dr. Bugsy. "Let's get a look at ya." He shined a light into my mouth and eyes and asked me to follow his fingers back and forth. Then I was sent for x-rays. They wheeled me back to my cubicle and laid me back on the bed.

"I want to try to get up." I said. Dr. Bugsy and Uncle Hunter helped me up off the bed and I took a few steps.

"I think he'll be fine," Dr. Bugsy said. "I'd like to admit him overnight and keep him under observation just in case, but I'm sure that the way he's moving our worst-case scenario is going to be a fracture or two. He'll definitely be sore."

It took some time for them to get me up to a room. Once I was settled Uncle Hunter offered to go call home and let Dad and Grandma know what was going on.

"I'll run back to the house and grab a few things for us, and I'll be right back." Mom said when Uncle Hunter got back from making the call.

"No need," Uncle Hunter said. "Just give me a list and I'll get it for you."

"I'd like to have a word with you anyway," Dr. Bugsy said to Mom. He smiled back at me. "Be back in a moment, Gil. Want some chocolate or something?"

"York Peppermint Patty?" I asked.

"You got it, Pal. Tea?" Dr. Bugsy asked. I nodded my head and then stopped. It was still hurting. "I'll have them bring you some pain reliever too." He said writing something on his clipboard. Then he and Mom stepped out of the room.

There was nothing to distract me from the pain and my situation. On the good side, I was probably fine. On the downside, I was missing dinner at home. I tried to think about what had been on the board for dinner tonight. It was Wednesday. Nothing Mexican. That was Tuesday night. What was Wednesday? I tried to picture the dry erase board Mom used to write out the week's menu.

# 17

Dr. Bugsy came back to the room with a York Peppermint Pattie and a cup of mint tea.

"I'd better go let your uncle know what to bring back for us." Mom said.

"Mom," I said. "What was planned for dinner tonight?"

"Leftovers," Mom said giving me an odd look. "Wednesday is always leftover night."

"That's right." I said.

"Probably hit your head when you fell," Dr. Bugsy said. "All the more reason to keep you over night."

"I certainly knocked the wind out of myself," I said. "It was like taking that first big breath after being in the water for too long."

"Can you hold your breath for me?" Dr.

Bugsy asked lifting his wrist with his watch. "Start now." He hit a button on his watch, and I held my breath.

"Come on, Bianca," Uncle Hunter said pulling Mom towards the door. "I need that list from you." Mom gave me another look and then headed out of the room to catch up to Uncle Hunter.

I held my breath and watched Dr. Bugsy who stood there watching me and occasionally glancing down at his watch. Finally, I let my breath out.

"Two minutes," Dr. Bugsy said. "Not bad. Not bad at all. Do you like pizza?"

"Do rabbits like carrots?" I asked.

"Not really," Dr. Bugsy said. "They'll eat them, but they prefer clover, dandelions, and other greens. What do you like on your pizza?"

"Like my ideal pizza?" I asked. He nodded. "Ranch for sauce instead of the tomato sauce. Chicken, bacon, and onions. A root beer to drink it down with." Dr. Bugsy pulled out a small pad and wrote it down.

"Okay," Mom said coming back in. Uncle Hunter's on his way back to the house for a few things, so all we have to do is wait. What's this?" Mom asked taking the slip of paper Dr. Bugsy was handing to her.

"His prescription," Dr. Bugsy said. "To be administered as soon as possible. I'll stop in and check on you in a few hours, Gil. I have a few other patients that have been admitted."

"A pizza and root beer?" Mom asked reading the paper, and back at me. I just shrugged. "Well, who am I to argue with the doctor?" She went to call Uncle Hunter and ask him to pick up a pizza and some root beer.

"I like this." I said as I lay in bed watching a movie with Mom while we ate our pizza.

"The movie, or the pizza?" Mom asked not taking her eyes off the screen.

"Just…this…Just you and me," I answered. "It's nice just being the two of us."

"It's hard sharing your mother with six brothers huh?" Mom asked.

"And a dad, and a grandmother, and an uncle."

"I guess I never really thought about that," Mom said taking another slice of pizza. "I try to spend time with you boys when I can, but I never really thought about any of you needing one on one time."

"It's not really fair though, is it?" I asked. "I mean, you're amazing and all, but you're still only one person and now there's ten people who want your attention."

"You think I'm amazing?" Mom asked looking at me.

"Well, yeah," I said. "You know where anyone of us are at any given time."

"I just know you kids," Mom said. "Like when Dennis goes running off, I have a pretty good idea what he's going to go for."

"So how did you know he was at the register when we were at the home improvement store?" I asked.

"I just figured he'd be done with his shopping by that time." Mom said with a shrug.

"Do you know what his project is?"

"Of course," Mom said. "I know the important things about all my kids."

"Except our birthdays, favorite foods, and favorite colors." I joked.

"Your favorites keep changing," Mom said. "Last year your favorite color was purple."

"How'd you remember that?" I asked. "Because by the time I was able to remember it you changed it and for some reason I keep coming to red for you instead of yellow."

"And our birthdays?" I asked.

"I used to remember them, but you guys never wanted a big deal made about your birthdays, so I just put them in my phone's calendar and set reminders. Frees up my brain space for other important things like knowing when my third born has fallen out of a treehouse but told the doctor it was a tree."

"I'm gonna kill Gary." I muttered.

"Why?" Mom asked. "He told us you fell out of a tree."

"So how do you know I fell out of the treehouse?"

"Because there's a treehouse," Mom said rolling her eyes. "No matter how deteriorated the rope ladder was, I knew you boys wouldn't be able to resist the temptation."

"You were right," I said smiling sheepishly. "When Mrs. Richards told me about it, I went straight to the woods to look for it."

"Mrs. Richards?" Mom asked.

"The lady that used to live in the house," I explained. "She's my adopted grandmother at the nursing home."

"Oh," Mom said turning back to the television screen. "You mean Old Mrs. Lottie Ballard."

"No," I said. "Richards. Her husband was Gabe Richards."

"Yes, but her maiden name was Ballard," Mom said. "Most people still call her Lottie Ballard because they call the house the Old

Ballard House. Seems disrespectful to me, but it is what it is."

The next morning, I woke up feeling a little disoriented. I knew I wasn't in my room. I blinked a few times as the hospital room came into focus. I'd been having an odd dream about the sweetheart tree in our orchard. The initials were still floating somewhere just beyond my consciousness as I tried to force myself awake.

Suddenly with a start, everything came into sharp focus, and I shot bolt upright in bed. Mom was already signing papers for the doctor.

"We're just about ready to go," Mom said. "The doctor wants to look at you first."

"We have to go," I said. "I need to go to the nursing home. I have to see Lottie!"

## 18

It seemed like it took forever to get done with the doctor and get out of the hospital.

"How about a proper breakfast?" Uncle Hunter said as we got into the car. "There's a Waffle House here in town."

"I have to get to the nursing home." I said.

"We have time for breakfast," Mom said. "By the time we're done eating, visiting hours at the nursing home will have started."

Mom and I both ordered waffles with milk. Uncle Hunter ordered a breakfast bowl with a cup of coffee.

"So why are we going to the nursing home?" Uncle Hunter asked as I fidgeted in my seat waiting for him and Mom to finish their meals.

"Probably so Gil can tell Lottie about the

treehouse." Mom said.

"I want to ask her about the apple tree." I said.

"Oh that," Mom said. "I think I've gotten that figured out."

"Really?" I asked.

"There's most likely a raccoon in that tree." Mom said. "They like sweet fruit and will often climb trees to get to them. We need to put some aluminum sleeves around the trunk to keep them out." I slumped down in my seat.

"That's not what I meant." I said.

"Well, let's go see the old gal and get some answers." Uncle Hunter said picking up the check and standing up.

"Gil!" Lottie said when we walked in. "I wasn't expecting you until Monday afternoon." She was sitting at a table in the dining hall. One of the attendants was clearing her plate away when we approached her table.

"I had to come see you," I told her.

"He found the treehouse your boys built." Mom explained.

"Don't give them too much credit," Lottie chuckled. "My husband was concerned about their building skills and insisted on helping them."

"The rail broke when he leaned on it," Uncle Hunter said. "We're just coming from the hospital."

"Are you alright?" Lottie asked. "I didn't realize there was a railing."

"It looks like it's in worst shape than the rest of the house," Uncle Hunter said. "I think your husband may have allowed the boys to do the railing on their own."

"It's possible," Lottie said. "He was most concerned with the floor rotting through if the walls and roof weren't done correctly."

"Forget about the treehouse," I interjected. "I'm more interested in the sweetheart tree."

"Oh!" Lottie said her eyes lighting up. "You found the sweetheart tree."

"Yeah," I said. "L.B.+M.D. Was that you?"

"It was," Lottie said with a smile. She got that look in her eyes that grown-ups get when they're looking into the past. "Maurice. That was my sweetheart's name. Maurice Durante. He was the son of an Italian immigrant, and my father absolutely hated him.

"We had to meet in secret if we met at all and we always met under that tree. Maurice would slip in through the woods and come out to meet me there. One day he sent me a letter telling me to meet me at the tree and we'd leave and run away together. I thought it was all terribly romantic, so of course, I packed myself a small bag of clothes and hid it under my bed until the night I would run off with him."

"But you never did?" Mom asked. Lottie shook her head sadly.

"No," she said. "I never did. The night I was planning to meet Maurice, my father came to my room and told me I wasn't going anywhere. I had just decided that if he locked me in my room as he was prone to do, I'd just climb out the window. My poor father never thought his dainty little daughter could do such a thing. Then he said something that just broke my heart."

"What was it?" I asked nearly in a whisper.

"He told me that he'd already met Maurice at our tree and offered him a thousand dollars to leave town and never contact me again. And Maurice took it. I told my father I didn't believe him. I went to the tree and waited for Maurice."

"And he didn't show." Uncle Hunter said.

"He didn't show," Lottie agreed. Then she barked a harsh and hollow laugh. "My father let me sit out there all night waiting for Maurice. He didn't come to check on me until just before sunrise. He said he'd figure that Maurice was only after our money and if he had refused the money then Father would have given us his blessing."

"How'd you meet Mr. Richards?" I asked softly. Lottie smiled and looked at me.

"Gabe," she said with a sigh. "Oh, Gabe, he was such a kind soul. My father told him what had happened, and Gabe immediately came to comfort me and told me just what he'd do to such a terrible cad." Her eyes went misty again.

"You still loved him though." I said.

"I still do," Lottie whispered. "I loved my husband and of course, my children, but I never stopped loving Maurice. I still have such a hard time believing he'd leave, but there you are."

"There you go, Gil," Mom said. "Your mystery is solved."

"Don't get too lost in the past, my dear boy," Lottie said with a wink. "Your family has ownership of the property now. Make your own memories and maybe take some time to leave some mysteries for those who come after you."

# 19

Gary came running out of the house when Uncle Hunter pulled the car into the drive. My other brothers were right behind him. Dad came out too under the pretense of checking the mail. But I could see him watching me.

"You're not dead!" Baxter said throwing his arms around me and hugging me tight.

"Your twin connection didn't pick that up?" Uncle Hunter laughed.

"I think it only works for identical twins." Baxter said letting me go.

"Dad and I got the chicken coop moved," Doug said. "Come and see."

"Later," I said tiredly. "I want to lay down."

"Good idea," Mom said. "He needs rest."

"Dennis," Dad called from the mailbox.

"You have a package." Dennis separated himself from the pack and went to claim it.

"Must be your spores and heating pad." Mom said. We all went into the house. My brothers and I went upstairs, except for Dennis who went straight to the basement.

"What is that little imp up to?" Gary muttered as he followed the rest of us to my room.

"Probably his project." I said with a shrug. I kicked my shoes off and flopped onto my bed.

"Mom texted Dad saying you were stopping at the nursing home," Baxter said. "Why?"

"Oh!" I said. "I haven't told you." I told them about meeting Lottie and choosing her as my adopted grandmother and learning that she had lived in it her whole life until moving into the nursing home. I also told them about the sweetheart tree. Neither Gary nor I said anything about the treehouse.

"So, the initials are Lottie and her sweetheart, Maurice?" Sunny asked.

"And he just left?" Sylvester asked. "What a jerk!"

"Lottie still can't believe it," I said. "I kind of want to go back downstairs and look at the tree again."

"Let's wait until after dinner," Doug said.

"Get some rest. Mom will freak if you're up moving around too much today."

After dinner, Uncle Hunter went out with us to the tree. I ran my hand over the sweetheart initials. Most of my brothers stood back looking around at the other trees.

"I can see why they met here," Sylvester said. "It's so close to the woods. Maurice could just slip right from the woods to this tree." The tree branches shuddered. I stood still with my hand still on the trunk. Everyone else backed up.

"That tree just moved," Baxter said. "I didn't just imagine that, right?"

"Talk to it, Gil." Doug said. I at looked him like he had just lost his mind. Gary was standing next to him nodding. I turned back to the tree.

"Do you miss Lottie and Maurice?" I asked the tree. The branches all drooped.

"The tree is sad," Dennis said. We all turned to look at him. He just shrugged his shoulders. "It is." I turned back to the tree.

"Are you sad because of Maurice leaving Lottie?" I asked. The tree shuddered so angrily that Uncle Hunter rushed up and threw himself over me as apples rained down around us.

When they finally stopped we looked up at the tree.

"Uh...guys..." Sylvester said. We all turned to look at him. He wasn't looking up at the tree though. He was looking down at the ground where the apples had fallen. They had fallen to form a long X. It was about six feet long and about two feet wide.

"Back to the house!" Uncle Hunter ordered. "Now! Gary, Doug, get your father and bring out some shovels. The rest of you go back to the house and stay inside. No questions." We didn't argue.

Sitting in the front room with my younger brothers, Mom, and Grandma while Dad, Uncle Hunter and the older brothers out digging up the marked spot started to drive me nuts pretty quickly.

"I need a snack," I said heading for the kitchen. Dennis followed me, but no one else moved to stop or join us. I had just reached for the snack pantry when Dennis grabbed my arm and pulled me towards the kitchen door.

I looked over my shoulder quickly, and then the two of us slipped out the back door and made our way back to the apple tree. We stuck to the shadows as much as possible. The sun had mostly set and we were fine right up until we got closer to the apple tree. Dad had apparently brought out some lanterns and the whole area was lit up to help them see what they were doing. Luckily, they were so involved in digging that we went unnoticed.

"If we slip into the woods and come back around, we can get closer." I told Dennis. He nodded and we did just that. We came up behind a tree just outside of the light and sat there trying to listen.

"That's it!" Dad called out after about five minutes of us sitting there. "Stop!" Uncle Hunter, Doug and Gary stopped and looked into the hole they'd just finished digging.

"Dad." Doug said. He tried to say more, but he couldn't.

"Call the police, Ian," Uncle Hunter said. "I'll take these two back to the house." Gary and Doug didn't say anything. They just let Uncle Hunter lead them away. Dad turned away and pulled out his phone.

"The police?" I mouthed to Dennis. Dennis crept forward towards the hole. I guess I should have stopped him, but I was curious too, so I followed him. He got to the hole first and at first he seemed to be physically pushed back from it. Then he crept closer. I looked over his shoulder and let out an involuntary yell that caused Dad to whirl around.

"What are you two doing here?" Dad demanded. Someone said something on the other end of his phone. Dad quickly told them he needed police at our house and gave the address. He then explained the situation and listened to what the other speaker was saying.

While he was speaking, I saw Dennis reach into the hole and grab something shiny. He was standing next to me looking as innocent as ever when Dad had hung up and turned back to us.

"What are you doing here?" Dad asked again. "You need to get back to the house."

"We were curious," I said. "We didn't think..." I trailed off and gestured to the hole.

"Not how I'd like to introduce you to the unpleasantries of life." Dad muttered.

"I don't think we'll need therapy, if that's what you're worried about," I said. Dad just grinned and shook his head. "So, who do you think it is?" I asked looking back down at the skeleton in the hole.

"I don't know," Dad said. "But that hole in the skull says he was murdered."

## 20

I can tell you from experience that being the new kid in a school is the worst. Apparently, the best way to be the new kid at school is to find a dead body on your property. Everyone kept pointing us out and trying to ask Sunny, Baxter, or me about the dead body that was found.

Joey and Harold of course, had already heard all about it. They got permission from their parents to come over and visit the very next day as long as they told their parents the whole story when they got back home. I told them almost everything. The only thing I didn't tell them. The only thing I didn't tell anyone about is the shiny thing Dennis had pulled from the grave. The thing he'd given to me, which was in a small pocket in my backpack on the first day of school.

After school, Joey, Harold, and I went straight to the nursing home to visit our grandparents and tell them all about the first day of school. Kendra looked up and smiled brightly as we walked in.

"Lottie is waiting for you in her room," Kendra said to me. "Joey, Nick is in the community room, and Roger is out in the garden." Kendra led me to Lottie's room.

"Lottie!" I said when I entered her room. She was sitting up in her bed reading a newspaper. She looked up when I entered and smiled brightly at me. For a moment, I could almost see the young woman who was getting ready to run off with her sweetheart.

"I heard!" Lottie said. "You found a dead body!"

"Not just any dead body," I told her. "Dad got the police report last night."

"Did he now?" she asked. "So do they know who it was?"

"Yeah," I answered pulling a paper out of my backpack. "Dad made a copy for me to show you." I handed it to her. She took the paper from me and looked it over. The smile fell from her face and she looked at me.

"Maurice." She whispered. I pulled the shiny

object Dennis had pulled from the grave out of the small pocket in my bag.

"This was in the grave with him," I said handing it to her. "I thought you should have it." Lottie took the diamond ring from me and held it up to the light. Tears ran down her cheeks.

"He lied," Lottie said. "Daddy lied. Oh Maurice." She moaned and buried her face in her hands.

"I'm sorry, Lottie," I said rubbing her arm. "I didn't mean to upset you."

"Oh, dear boy," Lottie sobbed looking up at me. "I knew he couldn't have left. I knew he couldn't have." She cried a bit more and I just stood there awkwardly rubbing her arm and looking around the room trying to not look awkward.

Joey, Harold, and I walked straight to the treehouse from the nursing home. As we walked, I told them about my visit with Lottie, and I finally told them about the ring.

"So, he had intended the whole time to run away with her after all." Joey said.

"And it was actually a relief for Lottie," I said. "She'd spent her whole life thinking she'd moved on a little too fast from Maurice and that maybe she should have waited for him to return. Knowing that he had been killed, made her feel better about marrying Gabe, but she said she has some personal searching to do to figure out how she feels about her father and his betrayal."

"I think your apple tree problem is solved though," Joey said climbing the ladder to the treehouse. "Another town curse broken."

"Don't lean on the rails this time," Harold called out to us as we all reached the platform. "We don't need any more hospital visits this year."

"Gary and Uncle Hunter said that everything looks good. We just need to replace the rail and the ladder," I said pushing on the rail and letting it fall to the ground. "It's nice to finally have something of my own that I don't have to share."

"You're sharing it with us though," Harold said as he and Joey pushed another section of the railing off.

"That's different," I said. "Usually, I *have* to share. This is the first time that sharing is *my* choice."

# GIL'S MIDNIGHT APPLE RINGS

INGREDIENTS

Oil
4 Medium Apples
½ Cup Sugar
1 Tablespoon Cinnamon
¼ Cup Apple Sauce
½ teaspoon Vanilla
¾ Cup of Milk
1 Cup Flour
1 ½ teaspoon Baking Powder
½ teaspoon Salt

- Pour oil into pan until you have an inch of oil in the bottom of the pan and heat over medium high heat.
- Peel and slice apples crosswise into ¼ inch slices. Use a small circular cookie cutter to cut out the center.
- In a small bowl, mix together 1/3 Cup of sugar with 1 teaspoon of cinnamon.
- In a medium bowl ix together the applesauce with the milk and vanilla.
- In a separate bowl, mix together the flour, baking soda, salt, - and the left-over sugar and cinnamon.
- Mix the dry ingredients with the wet ones.
- Dip the apple rings into the batter and then into the oil in the pan.. Fry on each side for about two minutes.
- When they're done frying, place them on a paper towel lined plate of bowl to drain.
- Roll in the cinnamon sugar coating and serve immediately.

    Enjoy your midnight snack.

# ABOUT THE AUTHOR

J. A. Miller is a middle-grade fiction fantasy author. She lives in Tennessee with her husband and a flock of chickens. She enjoys writing the kind of stories she wished she'd had when she was younger and the kind of stories the kids in her Sunday School class enjoy reading.

**OTHER BOOKS BY J. A. MILLER**

*THE MAGIC DOOR: THE WORLD OF EUDOCIA

*HOW TO CHANGE THE WORLD WHEN YOU'RE 12

**THE TAWNY DELIS SERIES**

*THE CURSED COOKBOOK

Made in the USA
Columbia, SC
24 November 2024